Mr. Not

"I am so glad we each found our very own Mr. Perfect! After searching all summer, we finally ran into the most awesome guys for us! The guys we were destined to meet!" Stephanie exclaimed to her friend Kayla. "And just in time for the end-of-summer party!"

"Spill," Allie commanded. "I want to know everything about your dream guys."

"Mine is wonderful," Kayla assured them as they walked along the path toward the docks.

"So is mine," Stephanie said. She glanced at the pier.

"There he is now!" Stephanie and Kayla cried at the same time.

In horror, Stephanie realized she and Kayla were pointing toward the same guy on the pier. They were both pointing at Brad.

Oh, no! Stephanie thought. *Is* my *Mr. Perfect also* Kayla's *Mr. Perfect?*

FULL HOUSE™: Stephanie novels

Phone Call from a Flamingo
The Boy-Oh-Boy Next Door
Twin Troubles
Hip Hop Till You Drop
Here Comes the Brand-New Me
The Secret's Out
Daddy's Not-So-Little Girl
P.S. Friends Forever
Getting Even with the Flamingoes
The Dude of My Dreams
Back-to-School Cool
Picture Me Famous
Two-for-One Christmas Fun
The Big Fix-up Mix-up
Ten Ways to Wreck a Date
Wish Upon a VCR
Doubles or Nothing
Sugar and Spice Advice
Never Trust a Flamingo
The Truth About Boys
Crazy About the Future
My Secret Secret Admirer
Blue Ribbon Christmas
The Story on Older Boys
My Three Weeks as a Spy
No Business Like Show Business

Club Stephanie:

#1 Fun, Sun, and Flamingoes
#2 Fireworks and Flamingoes
#3 Flamingo Revenge
#4 Too Many Flamingoes
#5 Friend or Flamingo?
#6 Flamingoes Overboard!

Available from MINSTREL Books

FULL HOUSE™
Club Stephanie

Flamingoes Overboard!

**Based on the hit Warner Bros.
TV series**

Brandon Alexander

A Parachute Book

READING

A MINSTREL®
BOOK

Published by POCKET BOOKS
New York   London   Toronto   Sydney   Tokyo   Singapore

A MINSTREL PAPERBACK *ORIGINAL*

 A Minstrel Book published by
POCKET BOOKS, a division of Simon & Schuster Inc.
1230 Avenue of the Americas, New York, NY 10020

A PARACHUTE BOOK

 READING Copyright © and ™ 1998 by Warner Bros.

FULL HOUSE, characters, names and all related indicia are trademarks of Warner Bros. © 1998.

ISBN: 0-671-02124-9

First Minstrel Books printing August 1998

10 9 8 7 6 5 4 3 2 1

A MINSTREL BOOK and colophon are registered trademarks of Simon & Schuster Inc.

Cover photo by Schultz Photography

Printed in the U.S.A.

Flamingoes Overboard!

CHAPTER
1

◆ ◀ ◆ ◆

"That was awesome!" Stephanie Tanner's blue eyes sparkled with excitement. She scooped her long, wet blond hair out of her face as another wave rushed over her legs. She was standing knee-deep in the cold water, holding her surfboard.

"Totally," Darcy Powell agreed as she gracefully leaped off her board. "Want to catch another wave?"

Stephanie glanced up the beach, where their friends sat sunning themselves. She shook her head. "Nah," she told Darcy. "Let's take a break. Besides, we should give someone else a turn."

Darcy shrugged. "Okay, but I don't think anyone else will want to ride as much as we do." She gazed longingly out to sea.

Stephanie giggled. Her friend looked so . . . so . . . wistful. "You know," she teased, "the ocean will still be here tomorrow. I don't think it's going anywhere."

"Very funny!" Darcy swooped an arm through the water, splashing Stephanie. Stephanie squealed and splashed back, then called, "Truce!"

"The water may be here tomorrow, but I don't know if *I* will be," Darcy pointed out. "I've hardly gotten in any surf time this summer."

"Summer Sail has taken up a lot of time," Stephanie admitted as the two girls trudged up the beach. "But it's been worth it."

At the beginning of the summer, Stephanie and her four best friends all joined Summer Sail—a program at the San Francisco Yacht Club that taught teens how to sail. It ran in one-month sessions. Now that it was August, the third and final session of the summer was about to begin.

"It will be great to start up again," Stephanie continued. "This month we'll be crewing our own sailboats!" She glanced over at Darcy, but her friend seemed lost in thought. "Hello? Earth to Darcy?" Stephanie said. "Still riding that last wave?"

Darcy smiled sheepishly. "Guess so," she admitted.

"You guys looked great out there!" Kayla Norris exclaimed, tossing Stephanie a towel. Stephanie caught it with one hand and began drying her hair.

"We *felt* great!" Darcy replied enthusiastically. She wrapped a large green towel around her skintight wet suit.

"That towel looks like a strapless dress on you," Anna Rice commented.

"And your wet hair makes you look like Whitney Houston on the cover of her last CD," Allie Taylor added.

"I guess I should wear towels more often," Darcy joked. She paraded around the picnic blanket as if she were a model on a runway. "Anna, can you whip me up a few towel dresses?"

Anna was very creative and enjoyed making all sorts of things, including fantastic clothes to wear.

"I know," Stephanie suggested, "an entire towel wardrobe for—"

"For the summer collection, of course, dahling," Kayla finished for her. She and Stephanie grinned at each other. Even though Kayla was one of her newer friends, she and Stephanie thought so much alike that they could complete each other's sentences.

Stephanie flopped down on the blanket and let out a long, contented sigh. She loved being able to spend so much time with her friends during the summer. Sometimes she had trouble remembering what it had been like before they all became friends. Often she felt as if they had known one another forever.

Actually, Stephanie thought, *I've known Allie practically forever.*

She and Allie met in kindergarten. Then Darcy's family moved to San Francisco when they were all in the sixth grade. The three girls met Kayla and Anna the past summer and now all five girls were fast friends.

The past summer was when they started a tradition of sleeping over at Kayla's every Friday night. At tonight's Friday sleepover they were going to listen to the newest Zack and the Zees CD.

Zack and the Zees were the hottest new group on the music scene. Stephanie and her friends had actually met Zack in July. "I can't believe you actually went out on a date with Zack!" Allie said, sliding a CD into her portable player.

"What I can't really believe," Stephanie admitted, "is that I thought he had to be my perfect guy—my destiny guy. But he was totally boring!"

When the summer began, Stephanie had come to the conclusion that there was one guy meant for her. She also decided that this was the summer to find him—and she wasn't going to rest until she did.

Stephanie frowned to herself. So far her mission to find Mr. Perfect hadn't gone well. Before Zack, she had decided that Josh, her Summer Sail instructor, was her destiny man. Then she found out he had a girlfriend.

I'm zero for two, Stephanie thought. *I sure hope my luck changes soon.*

Darcy knelt down beside the cooler and rummaged around in the ice. She pulled out a soda and flipped it open. After taking a long swig, she sat back on her heels. She patted her surfboard. "So—who's next?" she asked the group. "Who wants a turn 'hanging ten'?"

No one answered.

Darcy laughed. "Well, don't all speak up at once."

"Sorry, Darcy," Kayla said. She popped a chip into her mouth. "But the last time you tried to teach me to surf I ended up getting clonked in the head with the board."

"And I spent more time falling off the board than being on it," Anna added.

"But that's just because you need to practice," Darcy protested. "No one gets it the first time out."

"I bet *you* did," Stephanie commented. She always admired Darcy's athletic skills because Darcy could make the hardest things look easy. Stephanie wasn't a bad surfer, but Darcy was a natural. A true natural.

Darcy rolled her eyes. "You should have seen me when I started. I was klutzier than Anna."

"Thanks a lot!" Anna laughed and kicked some sand at Darcy.

"I just don't get the big deal about surfing," Allie admitted. "I mean, it looks cool and everything, but the ride is over so fast. I'd rather sail any day."

"We'll be doing plenty of that," Stephanie declared. "Just as soon as Summer Sail begins again."

"I can't wait!" Kayla exclaimed. "Let's sign up

for the last session together. First thing tomorrow morning."

"Deal!" Stephanie agreed. She grinned at her friends mischievously. "You know the real reason I like sailing better than surfing?" she asked.

"What?" Darcy asked.

"Because there isn't room for *two* on a surfboard!"

Stephanie's friends burst out laughing.

"True," Kayla said. "And since you *are* on a mission to find your perfect guy, you are definitely going to need to have a place to put him. Like right beside you—on a sailboat."

"Mmm. Wouldn't that be the most romantic date?" Stephanie murmured, picturing it.

Of course, it would be sunset. The waters would be calm. The breeze would be light—not enough to destroy her hair but enough to propel the boat forward. As the sun dipped lower, it would begin to get chilly. Mr. Perfect would notice Stephanie shiver slightly, and he'd put an arm around her to keep her warm—maybe even give her his jacket to wear. Stephanie smiled. It was something out of a romantic movie. But there was one big problem with her fantasy movie—she had no co-star!

Stephanie sat up and faced her friends. "What

am I going to do?" she cried. "I know that my perfect guy is out there somewhere. But *where?*" She gazed at each of her friends. "I mean, the summer is almost over and I haven't found him!"

"We've still got a whole month," Kayla assured her. She held up her bottle of water. "Here's to each of us finding our very own Mr. Perfect."

The girls raised soda cans and water bottles in a toast. "To Mr. Perfect!" they declared together.

Stephanie sighed. "Whoever he may be."

CHAPTER
2

◆ ◀ ◢ ◆

The smell of sizzling French toast greeted Stephanie as soon as she entered her kitchen the next morning. She stood in the doorway and took in the scene. As usual, the kitchen was packed with people.

Stephanie's mother died when she was little, and her dad asked her uncle Jesse and their friend Joey Gladstone to move into the house to help him raise Stephanie; her older sister, D.J.; and her little sister, Michelle. Then Uncle Jesse married Becky Donaldson. A few years later they had twin boys, Nicky and Alex. All those people, plus the family dog, Comet, and presto—instant chaos!

Her uncle Jesse stood at the stove. "Hey, Steph," Jesse called over his shoulder. "How was the sleepover?"

"Fun. Where's Dad?" She wanted to tell him she was going to meet her friends at the marina to sign up for the final session of Summer Sail. In fact, she realized, glancing down at her watch, she had to hurry or she would be late.

"He and Becky headed out to the marina early this morning," Joey told her. He sat at the table, trying to keep the twins from knocking every-thing over. "Someone spotted a sick dolphin in the bay this morning. Your dad and Becky were hoping to interview the marine biologists."

Stephanie's aunt Becky and her father, Danny Tanner, co-hosted the morning TV show *Wake Up, San Francisco*. They always met really inter-esting people because of the show.

"Do you want some breakfast?" Jesse held a plate toward her. He had cut the toast into finger-sized pieces and sprinkled them with powdered sugar.

"No, thanks. Kayla's mom fed us."

"I'll take one," D.J. said as she hurried across the kitchen. She grabbed a French toast finger and headed toward the door.

"That's all you're going to eat?" Jesse asked.

"I'm going to be late for work. I'll grab something at the office," she answered as she disappeared through the door. D.J. was nineteen and working in an insurance office during the summer.

"I'll take what's left," Joey declared. "Bring on the grub!"

Jesse set the plate on the table. But before Joey could take a bite, the twins reached across the table and snatched up all the toast.

"Hey!" Joey cried. "You didn't leave me any."

Alex and Nicky laughed. Then they shoved the toast into their mouths. The twins were almost five years old. *Those two are so crazy*, Stephanie thought with a smile. Michelle called them the "twin terrors."

Michelle! Michelle isn't at the table. Uh-oh. Stephanie hurried out of the room and raced up the stairs. "Please let her still be asleep," she muttered, "not up hogging the bathroom."

She arrived at the bathroom and tried to turn the doorknob. "Locked," she grumbled. She heard the shower running. Horrible off-key singing came from the other side.

Stephanie banged on the door. "Michelle!" she called out. "Hurry up. I need to get ready to go to the marina."

"I'm going as fast as I can," Michelle replied.

Stephanie groaned. Michelle never moved quickly in the bathroom. "I give up," she said with a sigh, and walked downstairs to the living room. After flopping down on the couch, she picked up the phone and dialed Darcy's number.

When Darcy answered, Stephanie said, "Bad news, Darce. Michelle beat me to the bathroom, so I'll be a little late meeting everyone at the marina."

"Oh, Steph, uh, listen . . . I'm not going to go to the marina this morning," Darcy said.

Stephanie didn't believe her ears. "What? But last night we all agreed to sign up for the Summer Sail session this morning."

"I know, but . . . well . . . I totally forgot that I had already made other plans."

"What are you going to do?" Stephanie asked. She was surprised that Darcy hadn't said anything earlier. They usually told each other everything.

"It's just something I need to do. Look, I have to go. I'll talk to you later."

Darcy hung up before Stephanie had a chance to say another word. *That was strange*, Stephanie thought. *Why wouldn't Darcy tell me what she was going to do? And why didn't she invite me and the rest of the gang?* she wondered with a sharp pang. She felt a hollow, lonely feeling in the pit of her stomach.

Then she shook her head. *You're just being silly,* she scolded herself. *I'm sure she'll tell you all about it later.*

Stephanie shielded her eyes against the bright sun shining off the water of San Francisco Bay. She waved to her friends as she pedaled toward the bike rack in the marina parking lot. Anna and Allie were waiting for her on the porch of the huge white clubhouse. Stephanie locked her bike into the rack and trotted across the wide green lawn to the clubhouse steps.

"Hey, Steph!" Allie called. "Where's Darcy?" she asked, her green eyes concerned.

"When neither of you showed up," Anna added, "we figured you were together."

Stephanie shrugged. "Darcy said she already had other plans."

"Plans?" Allie echoed.

"What could be more important than signing up for the last session of Summer Sail?" Anna asked. The sun reflected off the baseball cap she'd decorated with red and blue sequins.

Stephanie shrugged. "I don't know. She

wouldn't tell me exactly what she had to do." Stephanie gazed around. "Where's Kayla?" she asked.

"She said she was going to go ahead and register, but I think she might be hunting down the Flamingoes," Anna told her.

The Flamingoes were Stephanie's worst enemies. She couldn't figure out what anyone—especially *boys*—saw in that snobby group of girls. But they were very popular and would do anything to stay that way.

Of course, it didn't hurt that they were pretty, rich, and *acted* sweet. But Stephanie and her friends knew that the Flamingoes' "nice act" was just that—an act. Most of the tricks the Flamingoes played were directed at *them*.

Stephanie rolled her eyes. "What have the Flamingoes done now?"

"Well, we can't prove it," Allie began, "but we think they did *this*."

She handed Stephanie a poster. It was a blowup of a newspaper photo of Stephanie, Kayla, Anna, Allie, and Darcy standing by their winning swan float from last session's flotilla contest. When the girls won the contest, the Flamingoes were furious. Stephanie wasn't sur-

14

prised that the Flamingoes would try to get revenge.

But this was so mean! Stephanie stared at the poster. It was designed like an old Wanted poster. "Fashion victims" was scrawled across the photo. Underneath it read: "The way they dress is a crime!"

"These posters are tacked up all over the marina," Anna informed her.

"This is so childish!" Stephanie exclaimed. She was so angry, the poster shook in her hands. "I'm going to have it out with the Flamingoes once and for all!"

She stalked away from the clubhouse.

"What are you going to do?" Allie called out.

"I don't know," Stephanie yelled over her shoulder. She was tired of the Flamingoes trying to ruin everything. Things had been bad enough last summer with Rene Salter as head of the group. But with Darah Judson as their new leader, the Flamingoes were worse than ever. Darah seemed on a personal mission to make Stephanie miserable—and Stephanie couldn't figure out why.

Stephanie neared the outbuilding where the boating supplies were kept. Beyond it was the marina and the docks. She picked up her stride, not waiting for Allie and Anna to catch up. She clenched her fists and swung her arms hard as she rounded the corner.

And slammed right into someone.

"Ooof!" she heard.

"Oh!" Stephanie exclaimed. They grabbed each other's arms, trying to steady themselves. When Stephanie caught her balance, she gazed up into the greenest eyes she'd ever seen.

The guy smiled at her, and only one thought filled Stephanie's head.

He's perfect!

CHAPTER

3

◆ ◂ ◆ ◆

"I'm so sorry!" Stephanie gasped. "I wasn't looking where I was going."

"Neither was I," the guy said. He gave her a crooked grin. Stephanie guessed he was a little older—maybe seventeen.

Stephanie realized she was still clutching his arms. She could feel the heat of embarrassment rise in her face. Then she noticed that *he* also hadn't let go! A blush crept across his cheeks, and they released each other at the exact same time.

Stephanie felt her knees wobble a bit. *He is* so *cute!* she thought. He was tall with jet-black hair that fell across his forehead.

17

"You seem to be in a hurry," he told her.

"I was looking for Flamingoes," she admitted.

The guy stared at her in disbelief. "You were looking for pink birds that stand on one leg?"

Stephanie laughed at his puzzled expression. *That must have sounded pretty strange,* she thought. "No, the Flamingoes are a group of girls," she explained.

"You mean like a club?" he asked.

"Yes. And they always wear pink, so they're easy to spot," she told him.

"I don't think I've seen anyone who matches that description, but then, I've been here only a couple of days. My parents rented a house for the month of August."

Stephanie could not believe her good luck. He hadn't met any Flamingoes yet! Whenever she thought someone was cute, one of the Flamingoes always tried to steal him away from her. Usually that was Darah Judson. So far Darah had tried to steal *three* guys from her. It was as if Darah knew that this summer Stephanie was determined to meet her destiny boy. Staring at this great-looking guy standing in front of her, Stephanie hoped that maybe this time would be different.

"Do your parents have a boat docked here?" Stephanie asked.

The boy shook his head, which made his hair fall into his eyes. Stephanie thought he looked really cute brushing it back. "I'm here because I heard about these sailing lessons." He reached into his back pocket and pulled out a flyer for Summer Sail.

"That's why *I'm* here," Stephanie told him. "To register."

"Really?" His eyes brightened. "Then I guess we'll be seeing each other."

Stephanie grinned. She couldn't think of a better way to spend the rest of the summer—on a boat with this gorgeous guy at the helm!

If she could keep Darah away from him, that is. . . .

Say something, she ordered herself. *You're not going to make an impression if you stand here like an idiot.*

"You said you're new to San Francisco," she said. "Where are you from?" *Okay, so it's not brilliant conversation, but at least it's a start.*

"I'm from Arizona. It's nothing like this there." He gestured at the broad expanse of the blue bay. "Maybe I'll be able to shake some of the dust off me."

19

"Arizona is supposed to be really beautiful," Stephanie said. "I've always wanted to visit there."

The boy's smile widened. "Well, the ocean is one place I've always wanted to check out, and now here I am. I can't wait to be on the water. Have you sailed before?"

"This will be my third session," she told him.

"Wow! You must really know what you're doing." His admiring gaze made Stephanie smile proudly.

"I hope I don't make a fool of myself while I'm on the boat," he added with a laugh.

What a great laugh! Stephanie thought. "You won't," she assured him. "And if you have any questions, you can ask me."

His green eyes grew warm. Stephanie felt her heart swell. *Like a sail that has caught the wind,* she thought.

"Actually, I have two questions for you right now," he said with a grin.

"Go ahead and ask," Stephanie encouraged him. When he grinned, two tiny dimples formed in his cheeks. She thought they were so cute.

"I'm Brad. What's your name?" he asked.

Stephanie laughed. "Stephanie. That question was easy. Is your next one going to be harder?"

She smiled at him. His eyes met hers. They stood there, gazing at each other, for what seemed like an eternity. Stephanie's heart flip-flopped the whole time. "What is question two?" she finally prodded.

"Oh, right," Brad remembered himself. "Where can I get a good burger around here? I'm starving!"

"That's an easy one, too," Stephanie replied. "The Galaxy Grill."

"Hey, Stephanie!"

Stephanie glanced over her shoulder. Anna and Allie were waiting on the path leading to the marina clubhouse. She turned back to Brad. "Those are my friends," she explained. "I guess I'd better go sign up for the Summer Sail session."

"One more question?" he asked.

Stephanie smiled. "That's one more than you originally asked for, but, sure, go ahead," she teased.

"Do you have a boyfriend?"

Her heart flipped over. *There could be only one reason to ask her* that, *Stephanie thought. He was definitely interested in her.* "No, I don't have a boyfriend," she told him.

His smile broadened and his dimples deepened. "In that case, I'm sure I'll have more questions for you later."

More questions? Stephanie thought. Her mind raced. She hoped they'd be questions like "Would you like to go out with me tonight?" Stephanie already knew her answer would be an enthusiastic yes!

"Great," she said, trying to sound cool. "I'll see you around," she added. Then she turned to catch up with Allie and Anna.

She was glad her back was turned to him so that he couldn't see the huge smile that was spreading across her face. She felt totally wonderful!

This guy was so easy to talk to that Stephanie *knew* it was a sign they were meant for each other. Fate was working after all.

"Who was that?" Anna asked when Stephanie reached her friends.

"His name is Brad. He's here on vacation," she told them.

"He's so cute," Allie told her.

"I know. He just joined Summer Sail, and I'm pretty sure he's going to ask me out," she said, barely able to contain her excitement. She linked one arm through Allie's and the other through Anna's. The three of them walked toward the marina clubhouse. "He asked me if I had a boy-friend," Stephanie reported.

"Wow, Steph, this is great!" Anna exclaimed. "I knew you'd find the perfect boyfriend before the summer was over."

"We need to find Kayla so I can tell her that my summer-long search for Mr. Perfect is over," Stephanie told them.

"Not so fast," Allie cautioned. "What about the Flamingoes?"

"Flamingoes?" Stephanie wrinkled her brow and pretended to be thinking hard. "You mean those silly-looking birds that stand on one leg?" She giggled, remembering how confused Brad had been when she mentioned the Flamingoes. Allie and Anna laughed, too. Stephanie felt so happy that she couldn't be bothered with con-fronting the Flamingoes about their stupid poster trick. Besides, ignoring the Flamingoes was the *best* way to get even with them. They hated being ignored more than anything.

"Hey! Maybe the Flamingoes won't sign up for Summer Sail this session," Allie said.

"Wouldn't that be nice," Stephanie agreed. Then the Flamingoes wouldn't be able to come anywhere near Brad.

"The Flamingoes not causing trouble for us?"

Anna questioned. "I think that's too much to hope for," Anna commented. All three girls let out a long, dramatic sigh. Then they broke into laughter.

Stephanie took in a deep breath of sea air. She loved the marina, and she thought the yacht club was one of the prettiest places in San Francisco. She was glad Kayla had suggested they spend their summer there. *Funny,* Stephanie thought, *how Kayla and I always agree on things like this.*

Stephanie, Allie, and Anna crossed the wide green lawn to the white clubhouse.

Allie shoved open the double glass doors, and the girls hurried inside. Sunshine streamed through the glass windows that stretched along one wall. Stephanie gazed out at the sparkling bay and the bobbing sailboats lining the dock. Everything was so beautiful. Everything was *perfect*. This was going to be the best session so far—she was sure of it!

"There's Kayla!" Allie said, pointing to a slim girl with blond hair at the registration window.

Kayla turned at the sound of Anna's voice. She smiled brightly. Stephanie, Anna, and Allie rushed over to meet her.

"You guys are *not* going to believe what just happened to me," Kayla cried.

For the first time, Stephanie noticed the excited flush in her friend's cheeks. "What?" Stephanie asked. "What happened?"

"I met the guy of my dreams!" Kayla squealed.

"How cosmic," Anna exclaimed. "Stephanie just met the guy of *her* dreams."

"No way!" Kayla's eyes widened with delight.

"Yes! Way!" Stephanie squealed. "I bumped into him—literally! Wait until you meet him. He is *so* cute."

"So is the guy I met," Kayla gushed. "He's seventeen and he has his own Jeep."

"Oh, Kayla, I'm so happy for us!" Stephanie wrapped her arms around Kayla. The two hugged tightly. "This is going to be so much fun," Stephanie told her. "Hey—maybe we can double-date!"

"Well, he hasn't asked me out," Kayla confessed, "but I completely get the feeling he's going to."

"I feel the same way. I mean the way he looked at me, the way he talked to me—it was like there was a *connection* between us," Stephanie explained. "That's how I know he's my destiny."

"Hey, guys, did you see this?" Anna asked.

25

She stood near a large poster hanging on the wall.

Stephanie, Allie, and Kayla gathered around her. The poster had a midnight-blue background with silver stars glittering across it. It read:

The Summer Sail
Under-the-Stars Midnight Cruise
Crew members and their friends
are invited aboard the cruise ship
for a night of dancing beneath the stars.

"How romantic!" Kayla said with a sigh.

"I am so glad we each found Mr. Perfect," Stephanie exclaimed. "Just in time for the party!"

"Hey, we came here to sign up for Summer Sail, remember?" Allie teased.

"Oh, right." Stephanie giggled. "But then I want to hear all about Kayla's Mr. Perfect. And I'll tell you all about mine!"

"I already signed up, so I'll just wait for you outside," Kayla said. "It's such a gorgeous day."

Stephanie, Allie, and Anna hurried to the registration window and filled out the papers. When they finished, they headed outside to find Kayla.

"All right," Allie said. "Spill. I want to know everything about your dream guys."

"Mine is wonderful," Kayla assured them as they walked along the path toward the docks.

"So is mine," Stephanie said, glancing at the pier.

"There he is now!" Stephanie and Kayla cried at the same time.

In horror, Stephanie realized she and Kayla were pointing toward the same guy on the pier. They were both pointing at Brad.

Oh, no! Stephanie thought. *Is Brad Kayla's Mr. Perfect, too?*

CHAPTER
4

◆ ◄ ◆ ◆

"*Brad* is your dream guy?" Stephanie asked. She stared at Kayla.

"That's right," Kayla declared. She furrowed her brow in confusion. "Is there a reason he shouldn't be?"

"Yes!" Stephanie cried. "He's my Mr. Perfect!"

Now it was Kayla's turn to stare. "We both met the same guy?"

"Looks that way," Stephanie said. All at once she felt miserable. She and Kayla liked the same guy, and that guy was Stephanie's Mr. Perfect! What now? Somehow Stephanie was going to have to make Kayla see that Brad was completely right for *Stephanie*. Then Kayla would give him up.

"You know," Stephanie began, "he talked to me for a long time. I think—"

"He talked to me a long time, too." Kayla cut her off. Stephanie noticed that Kayla's jaw was clenched tightly. "And besides," Kayla added as she planted her hands on her hips, "I saw him first."

Stephanie heard the challenge in her friend's voice. She saw it in her eyes. Stephanie wasn't used to arguing with her friends, but she wasn't going to give up Brad that easily. He was the best candidate for Mr. Perfect that she had met all summer! Josh Hogan had had a girlfriend, and then Zack of Zack and the Zees turned out to be really boring. No, Stephanie had to think of some way to get Kayla to back off.

"He *hugged* me," Stephanie blurted out.

Immediately she felt guilty. It wasn't true— Brad hadn't really hugged her. He just grabbed her so they wouldn't fall.

Kayla narrowed her eyes. "Probably to keep you from falling down when you banged into him." Kayla paused. "And speaking of that, he talked to me because he wanted to—not because he was *forced* to!"

Stephanie felt her face flush. Kayla was right. Brad *had* kind of been forced to talk to her when she bumped into him. "He already likes me, Kayla," Stephanie insisted. "Just forget about going after him."

"Well, I think he likes me!" Kayla cried. "I'm not giving him up!"

"Neither am I!" Stephanie replied, angry with her friend. "So I guess it's you against me. May the best girl win," she challenged.

"Don't worry, I will!" Kayla countered, her tone hard and angry.

"Hey, you two, calm down," Anna said, but Kayla had already spun around and stormed away.

Stephanie watched Kayla stomp up the path. Her heart sank. She didn't want to fight with one of her best friends, but she wasn't about to give up her shot at finally finding her Mr. Perfect either.

A wave of sound hit Stephanie as she burst through the doors of the Galaxy Grill. She was so lost in thought over the fight she had had with Kayla that the noise startled her. She couldn't think about anything else all afternoon. Now that it was dinnertime, she hoped Kayla finally realized that Brad was the guy for Stephanie.

The music blared over the loudspeakers, and kids shouted at each other across tables. Stephanie scanned the room quickly, hoping her friends hadn't been waiting too long.

She spotted them at their favorite booth—Saturn. Saturn was a round table with a glowing neon ring around it. Neon stars twinkled on the ceiling and all around the booth. Anna and Allie waved at her from inside the flashing bands of blue and gold.

"You're late again," Anna commented as Stephanie slipped in between Darcy and Allie. As she settled herself in, she glanced at Kayla, ready to give her a friendly smile. But Kayla barely acknowledged her. Stephanie tried to shake off her friend's rudeness.

"Uh—sorry, guys. This lateness thing is getting to be a habit," Stephanie confessed. "This morning it was because of Michelle. Now it's because the twins hid my wallet." She smiled. "One of the many hazards of living in a full house."

Stephanie noticed that Darcy was reading a surfing magazine.

"Hey, Darce," Stephanie said, "we missed you today."

31

Darcy looked up and a smile spread across her face. "Thanks, Steph."

Stephanie was glad to see Darcy. "Don't forget that tomorrow is the last day to sign up for Summer Sail," Stephanie reminded her friend.

Darcy glanced away. She stuffed the magazine into her denim backpack. "Yeah, I know."

Silence fell across the table. Moments passed. No one said anything.

This isn't like us, Stephanie thought. *Why aren't we all talking and laughing like we usually do?*

She wanted to ask Darcy what she'd done all day, but Darcy was examining her fingernails as though she didn't want to talk. Stephanie wanted to talk about Brad, but she didn't want to argue with Kayla.

"Um—hey," Kayla said, breaking the silence. "Did you hear about the dolphin that's trapped in the bay?"

Stephanie wondered if Kayla felt as uncomfortable as she did.

"It was on the news this morning," Kayla added.

Stephanie nodded. "It's awful," she said. When her father drove her to the Galaxy Grill, he told her about his recent interview with the marine biologists. "As far as they can tell, the dolphin is all alone," Stephanie filled her friends in. "Marine biologists think he's sick. They tried to catch him so they could treat him, but he swam away."

"Poor thing! Alone *and* sick. He must be frightened!" Anna exclaimed.

"I wish we could do something to help," Allie said.

"Maybe when we're out sailing, we can look for him," Stephanie suggested.

"That would be great," Kayla said. For a moment Stephanie felt really good. She and Kayla were in sync again.

Anna and Allie nodded in agreement. Then the table fell silent again.

This is so weird, Stephanie thought. *I've never had trouble talking to my friends. Why can't I just tell them what I'm thinking?*

Stephanie glanced around the Galaxy Grill, trying to think of something to say. She groaned when she saw Darah Judson, Tiffany Schroeder, Cynthia Hanson, Tina Brewer, and Mary Kelly walk through the door. They all wore pink shorts and T-shirts with pink flamingoes embroidered on them.

"Flamingo alert," Stephanie whispered.

The Flamingoes sauntered through the Galaxy Grill as if they owned the place. Stephanie grimaced when she realized they were heading straight toward her table. Darah smoothed her hand over her long, auburn curls. She looked great—as usual.

"Check it out, an entire table full of fashion don'ts," Darah announced.

Tiffany Schroeder giggled. "I'm surprised you haven't been arrested by the fashion police. I heard they're looking for you."

"Not funny," Stephanie replied. "And neither were those fake Wanted posters of us you put up at the marina."

Darah tilted up her nose. "Why, Stephanie, I'm surprised at you! Accusing us when you have absolutely no proof!" A wicked smile spread across Darah's movie-star-pretty face.

"You're the only teenagers we know who act like they're six," Kayla said.

Stephanie was thrilled to have Kayla back her up. It felt good to be on the same side.

"Come on, Tiffany," Darah said. "Let's get out of here. Bad taste might be contagious."

"If it is, we caught it from you," Stephanie countered.

Darah rolled her eyes and wove through the

crowd. Mary, Tiffany, Tina, and Cynthia followed her to a table on the other side of the Galaxy.

Stephanie smiled at Kayla. "We sure told them."

"They are so rude," Kayla complained. "I wish we could put them in their places once and for all."

Stephanie glanced at Darcy. Plotting to put the Flamingoes in their places was usually Darcy's favorite topic of discussion. "What do you think, Darce? What should we do about the Flamingoes?"

Darcy shrugged. She continued staring at her fingernails. "Why don't we just leave them alone?"

"Leave them alone?" Kayla asked in disbelief. "Were you sitting somewhere else a few minutes ago? Didn't you hear what they said to us?"

"Big deal. They're just words. They can't hurt us." Darcy sipped her chocolate shake.

Stephanie stared at Darcy in confusion. Darcy was acting totally weird. The Flamingoes bugged Darcy as much as they bugged Stephanie— maybe even more. But today Darcy didn't seem to care at all.

"You weren't at the marina today," Anna told

Darcy. "You didn't see the mean posters they put up all over the place."

"It's like Kayla said," Darcy explained. "They're acting like babies. I have more important things to do than plan ways to get even with the Flamingoes."

Stephanie's mouth dropped open in complete shock. "Like what?" Stephanie asked. "What could you possibly have to do that's more important than getting the Flamingoes off our backs?"

Darcy reached for her magazine and set it on the table. On the front of the magazine was a picture of a guy surfing with a huge wave curled high over his head.

"Things like surfing," Darcy admitted.

Stephanie laughed. "Darce, sailing takes up most of our time during the day," Stephanie pointed out. "When are you going to surf?"

Darcy shrugged.

Allie stared at the magazine. She shook her head. "I guess surfing's not for me—I just don't get it. I don't see the appeal."

"I do," Anna said. She pointed at the guy on the cover of the magazine. "He's the allure!"

The girls all laughed, and Stephanie began to

relax. Things were beginning to feel normal again.

"He could definitely be *my* Mr. Right," Darcy said as she put the magazine away. "Now we just have to find Steph's."

"Hey! I knew I had something to tell you! I found him today," Stephanie blurted out.

She slapped her hand over her mouth when she saw Kayla stiffen in her seat. She wished she'd kept her mouth shut.

Darcy perked up. "Really? You met your Mr. Perfect? Who is he? What's he like?"

"Well . . . um . . . he's got black hair and green eyes." Stephanie glanced at Kayla. Kayla didn't look happy.

"I'll tell you about him," Kayla interrupted. "He's the guy of *my* dreams. As a matter of fact, *Brad* might be here tonight."

Stephanie's eyes widened. "What?"

Kayla smiled. "That's right. Brad asked me where he could find a good burger, and I told him to come here."

"He asked me the same thing," Stephanie told her, feeling a little satisfaction. She couldn't resist adding, "I guess maybe Brad didn't trust your answer."

"Guys, please, just stop," Anna begged.

"What's going on?" Darcy asked. "Are you two fighting?"

"They each met their dream guy today," Anna explained. "But it's the *same* guy!"

"No way!" Darcy cried. "You both like the same guy?"

"Seems that way," Stephanie muttered.

"He hasn't asked either one of them out, but they both think he likes them," Allie added.

"He does like me," Kayla said. "And you'll all see that when he asks me out first."

"*If* he asks you out first," Stephanie corrected her.

"Oh, don't worry," Kayla assured Stephanie. "He will."

Stephanie glared at Kayla through narrowed eyes. Friend or not, Stephanie was going to make sure that Kayla would lose this challenge.

Where Brad was concerned, Stephanie vowed, *Kayla's not going to have a chance.*

CHAPTER
5

◆ ◀ ◗ ◆

What am I going to do? Stephanie wondered. She sat on the edge of the dock the next morning, kicking her feet through the water. She felt so mixed up!

It just didn't feel right to compete with Kayla for a guy. *I should just let her have him,* she thought. *Or she should let me have him. But it doesn't seem like that's ever going to happen.* She sighed. *If Brad asks Kayla out,* Stephanie wondered, *will I hate her?*

How will Kayla feel if Brad dates me? Will she remain my friend? She shook her head. This was all so confusing!

The bright light dimmed as a shadow fell

across Stephanie. She glanced over her shoulder and her eyes widened.

Brad stood smiling at her, his tan face setting off his perfect green eyes. He looked so hand-some grinning down at her that Stephanie felt her heartbeat quicken.

"Hi," he said. "Can I sit here?" He pointed to the empty spot on the dock beside Stephanie.

Stephanie swallowed, hoping her voice would come out normal. "Sure."

She wondered briefly what Kayla would think if she saw Brad sitting with her. Her stomach knotted with nerves.

Then another terrible thought occurred to her. What if Brad started asking her about Kayla?

Brad set his bottle of juice on the dock and then dropped down beside her. They were both wearing shorts, and Stephanie focused on their tanned legs swinging in unison over the edge of the wooden dock.

"You're here early," he said.

"So are you," she pointed out. She rolled her eyes. *Try to be a little more witty, Steph,* she scolded herself, *or you won't stand a chance against Kayla.*

"I'm a little nervous—being the new kid on the boat," Brad confessed. "I'm afraid I'll make a fool of myself. I'm not sure what the difference is between the stern and the back of the boat."

"We all felt that way at first." Stephanie gave him an understanding smile. "But we all learned pretty quick that the stern and the back of the boat are the same thing."

He cringed. "See what I mean? I will look *so* dumb."

"You won't," she assured him. "Everyone in Summer Sail is pretty nice." *Everyone except the Flamingoes*, Stephanie added to herself.

Brad peered at Stephanie. "Hey! What's *starboard* mean? I always hear the word in movies, but I never know what it means."

"When you're on board, looking toward the front, or bow, of the boat, starboard is on your right and port is on your left," she explained.

"So if someone spots a shark on the starboard side, I should haul it over to the port side?" he asked, grinning.

"Definitely." Stephanie laughed. "You see," she teased, "you already know how to handle yourself in an emergency."

Brad laughed. *We are both totally enjoying ourselves*, Stephanie realized. *It really is like we're perfect for each other.*

"I don't think you'll see a shark," Stephanie

added, "but you might see a dolphin. There's one trapped in the bay."

"Hey, yeah! I heard about that on *Good Morning, San Francisco*. The marine biologists were telling people to keep an eye out for him," Brad said. "They were broadcasting the show from inside the marina. It was really cool to watch."

Stephanie felt herself blush with pride. "That was my dad's interview. He and my aunt Becky are the hosts of the show."

Brad raised his eyebrows. "Really? I'm impressed!" he said. "I know someone famous."

"*They're* famous. I'm not," Stephanie corrected Brad. She felt like she could talk to him all day. She glanced at their feet. They were swinging in perfect rhythm together.

"Stephanie?" Brad asked.

It was the first time he'd said her name. She liked the way his deep voice sounded.

"What?" she asked lightly, hoping he couldn't hear her heart thudding in her chest.

"My parents are throwing a beach party Friday night. Want to come?" he asked.

Stephanie felt her thudding heart race with excitement. He asked her to come to his party. That was a date! Okay, so his whole family would be there, but it was still a date.

"Sure! I'd love to come!" Stephanie answered.

"Great. We're staying in that big white house in the cove just before you get to Black Sand Beach."

"I know the one. It has a crow's nest, doesn't it?"

Stephanie admired that feature of the house many times. The tiny room with windows on all sides sat on the roof of the house. "I always thought a crow's nest would be the perfect place to sit and think," she added.

"It's my favorite part of the house," Brad admitted. "I like to go up there late at night and listen to the surf." He blushed slightly. "Last night when I was up there, I thought about bumping into you yesterday. I felt like such a klutz. I'm sorry."

He had thought about her last night? Happiness surged through Stephanie. Then something occurred to her. Had he thought about Kayla, too? She thought of asking, then decided not to bring it up. The only thing that mattered was that Brad thought about *her!*

"Don't apologize," Stephanie insisted. "It was *my* fault. *I* bumped into you!"

"I'm glad you did." He smiled at her. "Otherwise we might never have met."

Stephanie could feel herself beaming with happiness. She wasn't shy or embarrassed at all—she felt completely comfortable. Stephanie knew for sure that Brad was her Mr. Perfect. And he had asked her out! She hoped Kayla wouldn't have any hard feelings when she found out.

Footsteps pounded on the dock. Stephanie turned her head and saw Allie, Anna, and Kayla headed toward them.

"Here's the rest of the gang," Stephanie told Brad as she stood.

He scrambled up to help Stephanie to her feet. She couldn't stop herself from smiling. It was as if her grin had completely taken over her face. Brad was standing so close to her—like they were a couple!

Wait until her friends heard that Brad asked her to go to the beach party with him! *Please be happy for me, Kayla*, she thought. *I'd be happy for you.* Or at least she thought she would be.

Kayla sprinted down the dock ahead of Anna and Allie. When she reached them, Kayla smiled brightly. "Hi, Brad. You ready for your first day of Summer Sail?"

She didn't even say hi to me, Stephanie realized. *She doesn't have to ignore me and pretend I'm not here.*

44

"I think I'm ready," Brad replied. "Stephanie was explaining some of the fine points to me."

Kayla narrowed her eyes at Stephanie.

She's not happy, Stephanie thought. *She's going to become even less happy when she finds out that Brad and I have a date.*

She decided to break the news to Kayla when they were alone because she knew that Kayla would be hurt, and she didn't want to tell her in front of everyone.

Allie and Anna arrived at the end of the dock. "Hey, Steph!" they shouted.

"Anna, Allie," Kayla said quickly, "this is Brad."

"Hi," Brad greeted them.

"Ready to sail?" Anna asked the group.

Brad shrugged. "As ready as I'll ever be, I guess."

"We should go get our life jackets," Allie suggested.

"Shouldn't we wait for Darcy?" Stephanie protested.

"She's not coming," Kayla informed her. "She said she had something else to do."

"But it's the first day of Summer Sail," Stephanie said. "What else could she have to do? She should be here."

"That's what I told her," Kayla said. "But she said something came up and she'd see us later."

See us later? Stephanie couldn't believe it. She didn't want to start the third and last session of Summer Sail without Darcy. It just wouldn't be the same.

Why isn't she here? she wondered.

Stephanie played the scene from the Galaxy Grill over in her head. Darcy seemed all right. Then she remembered how weird Darcy got after everyone talked about surfing. Most of the time, Darcy surfed by herself. A lot of times, she even went surfing at six o'clock in the morning. She said the waves were really good then. No one seemed interested in surfing with her—especially not at the crack of dawn. But Stephanie knew doing things alone wasn't much fun.

We've all been so caught up in sailing that we didn't realize that Darcy wants to do something different once in a while. Maybe we hurt her feelings. I'll call her tonight and ask her if she'd like to go surfing together, Stephanie decided.

With a plan of action in mind, she shoved her doubts away. "Well, let's get our gear together, then," she told the others.

"Let the fun begin!" Anna cried.

"Speaking of fun," Brad said, "my parents are

throwing a beach party Friday evening. You're all invited."

Stephanie's heart dropped. Brad was inviting *everyone* to his party. He hadn't really asked Stephanie out at all. She tried to feel happy that her friends would be at the party with her, but all she really felt was disappointment.

Stephanie's stomach tightened. *That* meant he still might ask Kayla out first.

"Listen up, everyone!" announced a tall, blond college-age boy.

"That's Josh Hogan," Stephanie explained to Brad. "He's the head counselor of Summer Sail." She smiled, remembering that during the first Summer Sail session she thought Josh was her Mr. Perfect—that was until she discovered he had a gorgeous girlfriend. Now Josh and Stephanie were very good friends.

Everyone gathered around Josh. Stephanie scanned the group. It looked as though most of the thirty kids from the last session had signed up again.

Stephanie felt Brad's hand brush against her arm. He was standing very close to her. But Stephanie couldn't help noticing that Kayla hovered close on his other side.

47

"During this last session, you'll spend a few hours each morning on the *Sunshine* for class," Josh announced. "And then you'll spend the rest of the day crewing the marina's smaller sailboats on your own. Except for today, you'll spend the whole day in your own sailboat."

Everyone cheered and clapped. Stephanie was thrilled that they would be spending so much time handling their own boats.

Josh held up a hand. "But—as usual—there are some very specific rules I want you to follow."

"Wait!" someone cried. Stephanie knew that voice. She glanced over her shoulder. Darah Judson and her friends were strolling down the dock. They were always the last to arrive because they loved making entrances.

Stephanie rolled her eyes. Each Flamingo wore identical white shorts and shirts that showed off their tans. Pink anchors had been embroidered on the shoulders of the shirts. Darah wore a captain's hat over her auburn hair. Tina, Tiffany, and Cynthia had on bright pink headbands. Stephanie was surprised that Mary Kelly was missing. Usually the Flamingoes traveled in a pack—or flocks, Stephanie corrected herself, and stifled a giggle.

Brad leaned close to Stephanie and whispered, "Are those the Flamingoes?"

She shifted her gaze to him. "Sure are." She hoped he wasn't impressed by the Flamingoes.

Sure, the girls looked great, but underneath their pretty surfaces, their personalities were pretty nasty.

Darah elbowed her way through the crowd until she was at the front. "Thank you for waiting, Josh. You know how much we love Summer Sail," Darah said, smiling brightly.

Stephanie shook her head. During the first session of Summer Sail, Darah had liked Josh as much as Stephanie had. She tried every nasty trick in the book to get his attention. And even after she found out that Josh had a girlfriend, Darah *still* flirted with him. She never seemed to notice that Josh wasn't interested.

"Try to be on time from now on," Josh told Darah, and then glanced down at his clipboard. "The rules are simple. Five people on each sailboat. We'll mix experienced with less experienced crew members. Steer clear of the other boats as you leave the harbor. When you get out into the bay, keep within sight and yelling distance of one another. That way, if anyone runs into trouble, there will be someone nearby

49

to help. The counselors will be patrolling in powerboats. Feel free to wave us over. Any questions?"

Darah's hand shot into the air, but she didn't wait for Josh to call on her. "Can we pick our own sailing teams?" she asked.

"You bet. I want you to sail with people you trust," Josh explained. "As long as at least half your crew has completed the first two sessions."

Darah scanned the crowd. Stephanie knew that Darah was scouting for cute guys. *Oh, no!* Stephanie thought. *What if she asks Brad to be on her team? That would be typical.*

Well, there's no way I'm going to let her, Stephanie decided. "So, Brad, do you want to be on our team?" she asked quietly.

Brad's face shone with a delighted smile. "Great!" he exclaimed. "Thanks for asking. I was afraid this would be like choosing teams in grade school. It would be terrible to be the last one picked."

Stephanie laughed. "I don't think you'd have anything to worry about," she assured him.

"No, but you do," he replied. "I hope I don't capsize the boat!"

Everyone else quickly picked team members.

After Josh assigned each team to a sailboat, Brad raised his hand.

"My family is new to the area. I'd like to invite everyone to a party at our house Friday night," Brad announced. Everyone clapped and cheered.

Stephanie felt a flicker of disappointment. Now *everyone* would be there—including the Flamingoes! She'd be lucky to get Brad to herself once the entire night.

"All right, everyone!" Josh yelled, waving a hand in the air to silence the applause. "Be sure to put on your life jackets before you climb into the sailboat!"

Stephanie, Kayla, Anna, Allie, and Brad each grabbed a life jacket from the bundle on the dock. They headed to their assigned boat: *Princess Leia.*

"Is this boat named after the *Star Wars* movie?" Brad asked.

"Craig Walter, the head of the marina, loves movies. He names all the smaller boats after a character in a movie," Stephanie explained as they climbed on board.

The boat bobbed in the water. Benches lined each side of the boat. Allie sat on one side, Anna on the other. Stephanie and Kayla took places at the stern, while Brad sat next to Anna.

51

Josh and two other counselors, Fran and Ryan, walked along the dock, giving last-minute instructions. Ryan gave Stephanie a big wave, and she waved back and grinned.

During the first session of Summer Sail, Ryan liked her a lot, but Stephanie hadn't realized it. He spent most of the session teasing her. Steph thought Ryan was nice, but he didn't give her that breathless feeling she knew she should get from her destiny guy—her Mr. Perfect. Now she and Ryan were just good friends.

"This is going to be great!" Stephanie announced. "Sailing our own boat!" She felt her stomach flutter with excitement.

Brad leaned forward and rested his elbows on his thighs. He looked nervous. "I don't know how much help I'll be. I forgot to ask you what I'm supposed to do."

"Don't worry," Kayla cut in. "Since this boat is small, I'll be able to handle everything. I'll teach you as we go."

Stephanie jerked her head around and stared at Kayla. "You're not sailing this boat by yourself."

"That's right," Anna said. She nodded so hard that her sea gull earrings jingled. "We're a team. We work together to sail this boat."

"I didn't mean we wouldn't work together," Kayla explained as her gaze went around the group. "I just don't think we should expect Brad to do much his first time out."

"But I want to help. That's why I'm here," he insisted.

"Is your team ready?" Ryan asked.

Stephanie glanced up. Ryan was crouched beside them on the dock, holding a clipboard.

"We can't wait!" Stephanie exclaimed.

Ryan grinned at her, made a notation on his clipboard, and walked away.

Allie hopped out and unwound the bowline from around the mooring and tossed it onto the boat. After getting back in Allie pulled the line in, wound it into a figure eight, and set it in the bottom of the boat.

Ryan turned around and saw the boat slip away from the dock.

"Whoa!" Ryan exclaimed. "The mainsail has to be raised before you shove off! What's the matter with you?"

"Hoist the mainsail, Allie!" Kayla cried.

"Hoist the mainsail, Anna!" Stephanie cried at the same time.

Allie and Anna just sat and stared at each other.

"Well, who should do it?" Anna asked.

"You," Stephanie said.

"Allie," Kayla said.

"Anna is sitting closer. She should do it," Stephanie explained.

"Watch out!" someone yelled from another boat.

Stephanie glanced over her shoulder. Another sailboat slid past them, clearing them by inches.

"Get your mainsail up!" Ryan yelled again. "Now!"

"I'll do it," Brad said. "Just tell me how!"

"I'll show you!" Stephanie and Kayla cried at the same time. They both rushed forward and almost swamped the boat.

"You can't both do it!" Anna yelled. "Someone has to man the tiller!"

The current in the harbor had maneuvered the boat far from the dock. The crews on the other boats began yelling as the *Princess Leia* sat in the middle of traffic.

"Hey! Get out of our way!" Darah yelled.

Stephanie cringed. She felt ridiculous. She knew how to sail. It was Allie who unfastened the bowline. And, of course, it would be the Flamingoes who bumped into them.

"This isn't working, guys!" Anna said. "We need a captain."

"I'll be the captain!" Stephanie and Kayla cried in chorus.

"Out of our way!" Tiffany demanded in a loud, shrill voice.

Brad reached over and shoved the Flamingoes' boat away from theirs, but Darah still couldn't maneuver their sailboat around the *Princess Leia*. Stephanie and Allie grabbed the oars and began paddling the sailboat back to the dock, giving the Flamingoes room to pass.

"Looks like you're on a losing team, Brad!" Darah yelled as they glided by. "It's not too late to jump on our sailboat. At least we know how to get our sails up!"

"I'll stay here!" Brad called back. His gaze took in the other members of the crew. "We *are* going to get our sails up, aren't we?"

Stephanie couldn't think of a worse way to begin the third session of Summer Sail. All the boats were headed out into the open water of the bay, and they were just sitting dead in the water.

"Let's vote on a captain," Stephanie suggested.

"I vote for Kayla," Anna said.

"I vote for Steph," Allie said.

Stephanie felt as if it were the old friends against the new. She'd known Allie forever.

She'd met Anna and Kayla only the summer before. She looked at Brad. "You decide."

Brad shifted his gaze between them. "I don't know which one of you would be best." He gave a deep sigh. "I vote for Kayla."

"Kayla?" Stephanie repeated, disappointed.

He looked at Stephanie. "I'm sorry, Stephanie. I'm sure you're good. . . ." He trailed off and shrugged.

"Fine," Stephanie muttered, trying to cover her hurt.

"What's the problem here?" Josh asked as he approached in a small motorboat.

Stephanie was a hundred percent embarrassed. "Nothing."

"Do you need me to come on board?" he asked.

"No!" everyone on the boat shouted.

"We just needed to get our jobs straight," Stephanie assured Josh. She didn't want him to think they couldn't get their act together.

"And now that I'm captain," Kayla declared, "we're all set. Okay, crew, let's get under way. Umm, Stephanie, you take the tiller. Anna, Allie, hoist the mainsail as soon as Stephanie maneuvers the boat directly into the wind." She gazed up at Brad. "And, Brad, I'll go over all the things you're going to need to know."

Stephanie's jaw tightened. Kayla assigned her a job that could keep her farthest away from Brad if Kayla worked it right. And Stephanie had no doubt Kayla would.

Anna and Allie went to work and pulled on the halyard to raise the mainsail. It rose smoothly up the mast.

After the sail billowed out and caught the wind, the boat began to glide slowly through the harbor.

"Allie, hoist the jib," Kayla instructed firmly. Once the second sail was up, they moved more quickly through the water and soon caught up with the other sailboats.

Kayla and Brad sat side by side as Kayla explained the Points of Sailing; the orders such as "coming about" and "jibbing" and the names of various parts of the boat and the sails. Their heads were close together as Brad listened intently to her every word.

Stephanie gripped the tiller and fumed. The only reason Kayla wanted to be captain was to keep Brad all to herself.

If Kayla thinks I can't see through her tricks, she's crazy. Stephanie seethed. *Well, this isn't over. Not by a long shot.*

CHAPTER
6

♦ ◀ ◆ ♦

After the weird day on the boat with Kayla, all Stephanie wanted to do was phone Darcy. Darcy would side with her. If Darcy had been on the boat, Stephanie would have been captain, because Darcy would have voted for her.

She raced home from Summer Sail and immediately called her friend. "Darcy! Where have you been?" Stephanie demanded as soon as Darcy picked up.

"Surfing," Darcy answered.

"Surfing?" Stephanie repeated. "But you missed Summer Sail this morning."

"Oh, that," Darcy mumbled. "I didn't sign up."

58

Stephanie's mouth dropped open and she plopped down on her bed, stunned. "Why not?"

"I don't know. . . . I just . . . well, I'd rather surf."

"But, Darce, you can sail *and* surf," Stephanie protested.

"Not really," Darcy argued. "I'd have to get up really, really early to surf, or only do it on weekends. Summer Sail takes up so much time."

"But we're going out in our own sailboats this session," Stephanie continued. "We've been looking forward to that all summer."

Stephanie could hear Darcy sigh on the other end of the line. "Steph, I made up my mind. Don't give me a hard time about it, okay?"

"I'm not. It's just . . . well, we'll miss having you with us, Darce," Stephanie said.

"Hey, we can still get together. It's not like we're going to stop being friends," Darcy assured her.

"You're right," Stephanie said. She knew she was overreacting. "Listen, Brad invited us to a beach party Friday night. He lives—"

"I can't go, Steph," Darcy said quietly.

Stephanie paused. *Darcy turning down a party invitation? Weird.* "You can't surf at night," Stephanie pointed out.

"I know, but I'm doing something special and won't be home until late."

Something special?

"What are you doing?" Stephanie demanded. She used to know everything Darcy was doing.

"It's just something I've been planning for a while. Listen, I'm covered in sand. I need to take a shower. I'll talk to you later."

After Darcy hung up, Stephanie stared at the phone.

Five minutes. They had talked less than five minutes. Usually they talked for hours. And Stephanie had so many things she wanted to talk to Darcy about.

She wanted to tell her everything about Brad. She wanted to talk about how strange it felt to be interested in the same guy Kayla was interested in.

Stephanie lay back on the bed. It dawned on her that Darcy hadn't really told her anything—except she wanted to surf.

And she was doing something special—something that would keep her from going to a party. Darcy loved parties—what could she be doing?

Stephanie had more questions than she had answers.

What was really going on with Darcy? Stephanie felt as though her best friend were slipping away.

"I'll see you tonight, Brad!" Kayla called out.

They finished their sailing session Friday afternoon when they successfully docked their sailboat and stowed all their equipment. They had spent the morning learning how to respond to sudden changes in wind or tides. Then they took to their boats for what Josh referred to as "real-world" lessons. He explained that some lessons couldn't be learned in a classroom: how to make solid decisions and how to work like a team.

The only problem was, Stephanie thought, that she and Kayla were not behaving much like members of a team. They were both trying so hard to get Brad's attention that they were stumbling all over each other.

She watched Brad dash off to join a group of guys from one of the other sailboats. He turned and waved.

"You better all come tonight!" he yelled.

"We will," Stephanie promised. She was looking forward to the party. She had hardly had a chance to talk with Brad while they were sailing. They couldn't be distracted while they were in the bay with other sailboats around. The last thing she wanted—or needed—was to capsize or ram another sailboat.

"Don't you love having Brad on our boat?" Kayla asked. "He's so much fun."

"You mean he's so cute," Anna said, peering over her lavender-framed sunglasses.

Kayla laughed. "That, too."

That day had been worse than the ones before. Kayla had taught Brad the best way to catch wind coming from any direction. Somehow Stephanie ended up stuck at the tiller again and really felt left out when Brad laughed at the funny things Kayla said.

Maybe he did like her more, Stephanie thought, but she wasn't planning to give up without a fight. She had plans for the party.

"Hey, isn't that Darcy?" Allie asked.

The girls were walking to the far side of the marina. The shoreline stretched out to the side of them. Stephanie saw Darcy hurrying toward a nearby beach, a surfboard under her arm.

"Hey, Darcy!" she yelled. Maybe she could talk Darcy into coming to the party after all.

They all ran to catch up to Darcy, who looked ultra cool in her slick neon pink and black wet suit.

"Did you guys just finish sailing?" Darcy asked.

"Sure did," Anna said. "We really miss having you with us."

"Maybe Craig would let you sign up even though the session has started," Stephanie suggested.

"I've already made plans to surf for most of the month," Darcy explained.

"But surfing by yourself is no fun," Allie said.

"I have a surfing partner," Darcy assured her.

Stephanie blinked in shock. "You have a surfing partner?" Who could it be? And why hadn't Darcy told her this before?

"Is it a guy?" Anna demanded. "Do you have a boyfriend and didn't want to tell us?"

Darcy rolled her eyes. "No, I don't have a boyfriend. Don't you think I'd tell you guys that kind of news?"

"I don't know, Darce," Stephanie said. "There seems to be a lot you aren't telling us now."

"When did you get so obsessed with surfing?" Kayla asked.

"I've always loved surfing," Darcy said. "I never talked about it that much because none of you is very interested in it."

"I don't see why you can't sail *and* surf," Allie commented.

Darcy shook her head. "Trying to catch the waves around sailing was almost impossible. It was two months of craziness."

"I like to surf sometimes," Stephanie said. "Why didn't you ask me?"

Darcy shrugged. "You're totally into Summer Sail. I didn't think you'd ditch lessons to go surfing all day."

Stephanie bit her lip. Darcy was right. She wouldn't have skipped out on sailing just to surf.

"But I thought you liked sailing," Kayla said.

"Yeah, but I like surfing more," Darcy insisted. "Summer's almost over and I didn't want to lose all my wave time before school started." She glanced at her circle of friends. "Hey, look, guys. We can't always do *everything* together," Darcy explained.

"I'm not saying we have to do everything together," Stephanie told her. "But you're hardly around anymore."

Darcy smiled and said, "It's been just two days." Then she glanced at her watch. "Look, I need to run. Someone is waiting for me. We're going to catch the waves at Black Sand Beach."

"Near Golden Gate Bridge?" Stephanie exclaimed. "Are you crazy?"

"Do you know how dangerous the surf is there?" Kayla chimed in, concern on her face.

Darcy shrugged. "So the tide comes in a little fast. I'll watch out for it."

"You *and* your mystery surfing partner will watch out, you mean," Stephanie said. "So who is it?"

"Look, I really have to go." Darcy hiked the surfboard up under her arm, turned, and headed toward Black Sand Beach. "See you!"

They watched Darcy disappear down the beach. "Well, that was weird," Anna commented.

"It sure seemed like Darcy was trying to hide something," Allie agreed. "She acted like all she wanted was to get away from us."

Stephanie nodded. Darcy had never acted like that before. "Who do you think her surfing partner could be?" Stephanie wondered. "Do you think she secretly has a boyfriend? And why wouldn't she tell us?"

Kayla glanced at Stephanie. "Maybe she's afraid one of us will try to steal him away," she muttered.

Stephanie stared at Kayla—and Kayla quickly

glanced away. She noticed Allie and Anna make eye contact.

Does Darcy just not want to spend time with us anymore? Stephanie wondered. She had to admit things had been kind of weird between them the last few days.

Could that mean that Darcy has found a new best friend?

"Too bad Darcy's not here," Allie said to Stephanie as they entered the mall a half hour later.

"Yeah," Stephanie agreed. "Three heads are always better than two." She smiled at Allie. "But I'm glad you're here."

"How will I have time to find the perfect outfit?" Stephanie fretted. "There's not enough time before Brad's party."

"What kind of outfit do you want?" Allie asked.

Stephanie frowned as they headed for the escalator. "I'm not sure. Something that makes me look a little older. After all, Brad is seventeen."

Stephanie glanced around the mall. There was a lot riding on this shopping trip. Stephanie had to look *so* great that Brad would never notice Kayla—or any of the Flamingoes, either.

"Allie, who do you think Brad likes the most—me or Kayla?"

Allie narrowed her green eyes. "It's hard to say, Steph. He's nice to everyone."

Stephanie nodded. "I really like him, but I feel funny trying to get him to ask me out when I know Kayla likes him, too."

"But what can you do if he likes you more?" Allie asked.

"I don't know, Allie," Stephanie confessed. "Sometimes I can't help wondering if I should just let Kayla have Brad. After all, she is my friend."

"Or she could let you have him," Allie pointed out.

"That's true. I guess I should just go to the party and see what happens." She sighed. When did love and friendship become so complicated?

"So where should we start shopping?" Allie asked.

"Kaleidoscope," Stephanie suggested as they rode the escalator to the second floor. "I want to wear something totally cool."

They strolled into Kaleidoscope and Stephanie began flipping through a rack of brightly colored shirts.

"How about a broom skirt?" Allie held up a long, deep green skirt.

"Cool!" Stephanie always liked that wrinkled look, and she could wear it with sandals and a T-shirt.

She found a cropped T-shirt that was the same shade as Brad's eyes. "Look at this, Allie." She held the shirt next to the skirt Allie had shown her.

Allie's eyes widened. "Oh, Steph, you'll look great."

"This is perfect!" someone exclaimed behind them.

Stephanie recognized the voice—Kayla! She spun around. Kayla stood in front of a three-way mirror beside the dressing rooms. Her elder sister was with her.

Kayla was wearing the same broom skirt and cropped T-shirt that Stephanie had picked out. Stephanie's heart sank. The outfit looked great on Kayla!

Kayla twirled around, making the skirt billow out. Then she came to an abrupt stop and stared at Stephanie.

"Steph! I didn't know you were going to be here," Kayla said. "What do you think of my outfit?"

Stephanie shrugged. "It's all right, I guess."

She saw the disappointment in Kayla's blue eyes. Stephanie's stomach knotted.

Why can't I tell her the truth—that she looks great? Stephanie wondered. *Here I am, trying to make her feel insecure—just because I wanted to wear that outfit. I'd feel terrible if Kayla treated me this way.*

She had to be honest with Kayla. After all, she was her friend, and friends are honest with each other. "Actually, it looks great, Kayla," she admitted.

Kayla's eyes brightened, and she seemed relieved. "I'm going to find some earrings to match." She hurried into a dressing room.

Stephanie shoved her broom skirt and shirt back onto the rack.

"I need to find something completely different," Stephanie said to Allie.

"Yeah, too bad she beat you to the broom skirt," Allie sympathized. "You would have looked great in it."

Stephanie sorted through the outfits but couldn't find anything she liked.

"I'll see you guys tonight," Kayla said as she left the store, carrying a large sack.

Stephanie watched Kayla leave. She frowned

as ugly thoughts filled her head. She didn't want Kayla to look beautiful. She didn't want her to catch Brad's attention.

Stephanie shuddered. *I can imagine feeling this way about one of the Flamingoes,* she thought. *But I can't believe I'm feeling this way about one of my best friends!*

CHAPTER
7

◆ ◂ ◆ ◆

"Dad, there's Brad's house!" Stephanie exclaimed later as her father drove their car along the road into the cove.

Stephanie's eyes traveled up Brad's tall, white house to the crow's nest on top. A cozy warmth welled up inside her as she imagined Brad in that little nook, thinking about her. Beyond the house, the cliffs of Black Sand Beach blocked the view of the surf. The sun was just settling on the horizon.

"*This* is where he lives?" nine-year-old Michelle asked from the backseat. "Cool."

Her dad pulled the car to a stop. Stephanie felt a flutter of nerves because she wanted Brad to notice her so much.

She got out of the car, and her heart started pounding when she spotted Brad heading her way.

"Hey!" Brad called as he jogged over to Stephanie. "I thought you'd never get here."

Stephanie beamed. He was waiting for me!

Danny poked his head out the car window. "That was my fault," he confessed.

"Just as we were leaving the house, someone called and reported that he'd seen the dolphin," Stephanie explained.

"I was making arrangements to interview the marine biologists again in the morning," Danny added.

"I watched your broadcast from the marina," Brad told Stephanie's dad. "It was really cool. I'm going to major in television and film when I go to college next year."

Uh-oh, Stephanie thought. *Dad loves talking about his job. Please, please, please, don't launch into a long, boring story.*

"Why don't you stop by the television studios sometime, and I'll show you around," her dad offered.

Brad's eyes brightened. "Great!"

"Dad," Michelle complained. "Come on. Cassie is waiting for me at her house."

Thank you, Michelle, Stephanie said silently. Sometimes having a younger sister could actually come in handy.

"Yes, madam," Danny joked. "A chauffeur's job is never done. See you later, honey."

"Your dad is cool," Brad told Stephanie as they watched the car drive away.

"He can be," Stephanie agreed. "On a good day."

Brad laughed and led her around the side of the house.

"Wow! Everyone from the marina is here," Stephanie commented. She saw most of the kids from Summer Sail standing around and talking.

"You look great," Brad told her.

"Thanks." Stephanie felt herself blush. She never did buy anything at the mall. She didn't find anything she liked better than the broom skirt, so she finally decided to wear a favorite pair of bright blue shorts and a striped cotton sweater. Brad wore cutoff jeans and a green fifties-style bowling shirt. Stephanie thought he looked fantastic.

"How about a game of volleyball?" Brad suggested.

Stephanie followed him to a place on the beach where a net had been stretched across the sand. No one was playing yet, but Kayla, Allie, and Anna stood nearby. Stephanie felt a twinge of envy looking at Kayla in her broom skirt.

"I'll see if I can scare up some other players," Brad said before he strolled away.

Stephanie joined her friends. "Do you guys want to play volleyball?" she asked.

"You bet," Anna exclaimed.

"Brad already asked us," Kayla told her.

Stephanie bit back her disappointment. She hoped Brad had asked her first.

"How are you going to play in that long skirt?" Stephanie asked Kayla. Maybe Kayla would go hang out somewhere else.

Kayla put her hands on her hips and glared at Stephanie. "Don't worry about me," she retorted. "I'll do just fine."

Stephanie had been at the party only a few minutes, and already she and Kayla were sniping at each other. *If only Darcy were here.* Stephanie wished she could talk to her best friend about what was going on with Kayla.

Then she remembered why Darcy wasn't at the party. Darcy had plans with a new friend. Maybe Darcy wouldn't be such a big help after all. "Do you think Darcy is still surfing?" Stephanie asked.

"I doubt it," Allie answered. "It'll be dark soon."

"I got some players," Brad announced as he returned to the volleyball court.

Stephanie groaned when she saw Darah sauntering toward them. She wore tight pink shorts and a halter top that revealed her perfect tan. Tiffany, Cynthia, Tina, and six guys followed Darah.

"I wonder where Mary is," Anna commented.

"Since she's not sailing this session, maybe she'll be going on vacation somewhere with her family," Stephanie said. "Somewhere exotic like Bali or Paris."

Darah picked up the volleyball and tossed it lightly in the air. "Here's my team," she declared. "But we'll make room for you, Brad."

Brad laughed. "I'll play on the other team. Besides, we're using nine players on a team. You need to get rid of someone."

Darah gave Tiffany a sharp nod. "Tiffany, you're off my team."

Tiffany's eyes widened in horror. "But I want to play!"

"I'm not going to take any of the *guys* off my team." Darah gave the boys surrounding her a bright smile.

"You can play on our team," Brad offered.

Tiffany looked past Brad to Stephanie and her friends. "No thanks," Tiffany replied. "I'll keep score."

Stephanie shook her head. *Typical Flamingo,* she thought. *Tiffany would rather not play than be on our side.*

Brad cast a glance at Stephanie. "We need more players. Any ideas?"

Stephanie scanned the crowd of people milling around. "Josh."

"And Fran," Allie added. "She's really athletic. She should be a great player." Fran had been Allie's instructor during the first Summer Sail session.

Brad called them over. Josh brought his girlfriend, Stacy. Now Stephanie's team had eight players. Close enough. Stephanie kicked off her sandals and took her place in the front row between Brad and Josh. Kayla stood in the row behind them.

Suddenly the ball flashed by Stephanie. Instinctively, she jerked back. Anna shrieked and raced forward. Sand flew into the air, but it was too late. The volleyball landed with a thud on the sand.

"Our point!" Darah exclaimed.

"Not fair!" Stephanie yelled. "We weren't ready."

Darah gave Stephanie an innocent look. "I'm sorry. We thought you were."

Stephanie knew Darah always acted sweet when guys were around. It was one of the reasons they actually liked her. Stephanie glanced at her team. "Are we ready?"

"You bet," Brad said as he tossed the ball over the net to Darah. "You won't sneak another one by us."

The ball whizzed straight at Stephanie. She neatly hit it back over the net.

"Great shot!" Brad shouted.

A guy on the other side knocked the ball back to Stephanie's side of the net. Brad hit the ball straight up in the air, setting it up for a spike. "Get it!" Brad yelled.

Stephanie lunged for it. Suddenly Kayla was in front of her, jumping up and slamming the ball hard over the net. It landed on the sand between Cynthia and Tina.

"Don't you two know how to play?" Darah screamed at her team members.

"I thought Cynthia was going to get it," Tina cried.

"I thought it was Tina's ball," Cynthia yelled.

Stephanie turned to face Kayla. "What were you doing in my space?" she demanded.

"Helping us win," Kayla shot back.

"Hey, get ready for the serve!" Anna's voice snapped Stephanie back to the game.

Stephanie felt her face heat up. "We sound just like the Flamingoes, fighting with each other," Stephanie whispered to Kayla. "We need to play together if we want to beat them."

Kayla paused as if she were going to argue, but then she nodded. "You're right." She returned to her position on the court.

Stephanie breathed a sigh of relief. She knew they could win if they played together as a team.

She couldn't help but snicker to herself when she noticed Kayla hike up her skirt and tuck the ends into her waistband. Obviously Kayla was worried about playing in her long skirt, which didn't look very sophisticated anymore. Stephanie felt a lot better about not buying the skirt now.

"Give us the ball!" Stephanie called out.

Tina tossed it over the net. Stephanie caught it and threw it to Anna. "Come on, Anna, get us a point!"

Anna served the ball. It skimmed over the top of the net.

One of the guys on Darah's team hit it hard, sending it back. Brad leaped up and twisted, knocking the ball high into the air. When it came down, Allie slammed it back over toward the Flamingoes.

Tina hit it straight into the net. Some of the crowd that had gathered on the sidelines applauded.

"Yes!" Stephanie cheered. *Now, that's more like it!*

"Great teamwork!" Josh shouted.

After several plays it was Stephanie's turn to serve.

"This is game point," Brad reminded her.

Stephanie nodded and breathed deeply. She really didn't want to blow it. Her team—and Brad—were counting on her.

Stephanie took a moment to concentrate, then—wham!—she sent the ball sailing over the net. Darah slammed it back.

Stephanie kept her eye on the ball, every muscle ready to spring into action.

"I've got it!" Stephanie cried. She fell to her knees and knocked the ball into the air just inches above the sand.

"It's mine!" Anna yelled, rushing forward. She

lost her balance in the sand. Somehow she managed to hit the ball, but not very hard.

Oh, no! Stephanie thought. *It's not going to make it.*

"Mine!" Kayla yelled.

Stephanie heard the loud pop as Kayla slammed the ball over the net. Darah, Tina, and Cynthia scrambled for it, but missed. It landed on the sand.

"We won!" Brad cried, smiling broadly.

Darah gave Stephanie an angry glare. Stephanie knew Darah didn't like to lose, especially when guys were around.

"We'll beat you next time," Darah promised.

Brad smiled and draped an arm around Kayla's shoulder. "You were great, Kayla. You've got the best volleyball moves I've ever seen."

"I wasn't really dressed for a game," Kayla commented, glancing down at her skirt. She tucked some of the fabric more securely into the waistband.

"Maybe you'll start a new trend in volleyball wear," Brad joked. "Especially after we beat them again in another game."

Kayla beamed and Stephanie felt her heart sink.

Suddenly all Stephanie wanted was to get

away from the group. "Hey, I'm going to get something to drink," she called, and hurried to find the refreshment table.

Now she knew Kayla had been right. Brad did like Kayla best.

Stephanie grabbed a can of soda, then wandered down to the shoreline. She stood gazing out at the water. She couldn't help it. No matter how hard she tried to be happy for Kayla, she still wished Brad liked her.

"Beautiful, isn't it?" a voice said beside her.

Stephanie turned and smiled at Brad.

"It's so different from back home," Brad continued. "We've got nothing but sand everywhere."

"That could be kind of cool, too," Stephanie said, and sighed. "We should get back to the game." She turned to go.

Brad grabbed her hand, stopping her. "Wait! What's the hurry?" he asked.

"Don't you want to win another game of volleyball?" Stephanie replied.

"I'd rather spend some time with you— alone," he told her.

Stephanie felt her heart flip over. But she was also confused. "I thought you liked Kayla."

Brad looked surprised. "I do. She's teaching me a lot on the sailboat."

"I mean . . . I thought . . ." Stephanie didn't know exactly how to say it, so she blurted out, "Don't you like Kayla as a girlfriend?"

Grinning, Brad squeezed her hand. "I like Kayla a lot, but I like you more."

Joy shot through Stephanie. *Yes! He likes me more after all!*

He tugged on her hand. "Walk up the beach with me."

Stephanie nodded. She didn't trust herself to speak. She was afraid she'd start giggling like crazy. *Amazing*, she thought as they strolled toward the cliffs, *just a minute ago I was feeling sorry for myself. And now I am so happy!*

"Hey, have I told you I think you're a great sailor," Brad said.

"I'm just doing the things that I learned during the first two sessions," she told him.

She and Brad had walked quite a distance away from the party. She heard the waves pounding at the shore. In the distance she saw the sun sinking below the horizon. It threw an orange glow over the water. *Sunset must be the most romantic time of day for a walk on the beach.*

"Hey, look at this," Brad said. He reached

down and dug something out of the wet sand, then held it up. "A perfect sand dollar."

"Those are rare," she told him. "I've never been able to find one."

"You can have this one," he said, holding it out to her.

"You should keep it as a souvenir of your vacation here," she protested.

"I'd rather you keep it." He paused. "As a reminder of me."

Stephanie's heart thudded so hard, she was certain he could hear it. She knew she'd remember him—with or without the sand dollar. She slipped it into the pocket of her shorts. "Thank you."

Brad took her hand. She liked the way it felt to have his hand around hers. It was—perfect.

Everything was perfect. Brad was obviously her Mr. Perfect—the boy hand-picked by fate to be hers. *And I bet he'll ask me to the midnight cruise!* Stephanie couldn't wait.

"I like you, Stephanie." Brad bent his head slightly and tightened his hand around hers.

He's going to kiss me, Stephanie realized. She held her breath, waiting.

"Help! Help!"

Brad jerked his head up. They both looked

around, trying to figure out who was screaming. There was no one nearby.

The shouting came again. Stephanie pointed toward the cliffs. "It sounds like it's coming from Black Sand Beach!"

She and Brad ran toward the cliffs. The screaming grew louder as Stephanie glanced over the edge.

A girl in a wet suit was standing alone on the beach, screaming.

"Help!" she hollered. "Darcy! Darcy wiped out!"

CHAPTER
8

"I have to help Darcy!" Stephanie half slid and half raced down the cliffside trail leading to the beach. She ignored the dune grass that scraped at her ankles, only trying to remain upright. Her feet pounded straight down, scattering pebbles.

"I'm going to the house to get help," Brad called from behind her.

On flat ground now, Stephanie hurtled quickly along the wet sand. She slowed a bit when she recognized the shouting girl in the wet suit. It was Mary Kelly, one of the Flamingoes.

Mary pointed toward a jetty thrust out into the bay. "Darcy wiped out near those rocks!"

Stephanie kicked off her sandals and raced

into the water. *Where is Darcy? Why hasn't she come up yet?*

Stephanie gulped and dove into the ice-cold waves. Had Darcy been swept under? Had she banged her head on the rocks? Stephanie fought back her panic. The current was really strong, creating a powerful undertow. She and Darcy were both good swimmers, but if the board had hit her, or she swallowed too much water . . . Stephanie forced herself not to think about it.

She swam to where Mary was pointing, took a deep breath, and prepared to dive.

All at once Darcy's head broke through the surface a few feet away. She gasped in great gulps of air.

"That was awesome!" Darcy exclaimed.

Huh? Stephanie treaded water and stared at Darcy. *Darcy wasn't in danger! Darcy was having a great time!*

"Stephanie!" Darcy's eyes widened in surprise when she saw Stephanie. "What are you doing here?"

"I was trying to rescue *you!*" Stephanie replied. "I heard Mary shouting."

Darcy laughed and swam toward her. "That's really nice of you, but—see, I'm fine. In fact, I feel great."

"Yeah, but look at me!" Stephanie complained as they headed back up on the beach. She glanced down at her outfit. It was totally ruined. The blue dye in her shorts dripped along her legs, and the stripes on her sweater were beginning to run. Her hair hung in limp wet clumps.

But thank goodness it was just a false alarm! She shivered, just thinking about what could have happened to her best friend.

"Darcy, what were you—" Stephanie began as they reached the sand.

Mary rushed over to Darcy and threw her arms around her. "That was a major wipeout!" she cried. "Are you okay?"

Darcy nodded and laughed. "I'm great. Wasn't that the most awesome wave? I felt, like, practically pro out there," Darcy said. "How was my form?"

"Uh, great," Mary told her.

"You think so?" Darcy's dark eyes sparkled with excitement. "I held it as long as I could."

Stephanie stared at the two girls. *What is going on? Why is Darcy talking like this to Mary—a Flamingo? They actually sound like they're friends!*

Then it hit her. *Of course.* The matching wet suits, Darcy's secrecy . . . it all added up to one thing.

Mary Kelly was Darcy's mysterious surfing partner!

Stephanie couldn't believe it. Darcy had chosen surfing with a Flamingo—one of Stephanie's worst enemies—over spending time with her!

Stephanie's chest felt as if it were being squeezed tight. "Darcy, what is going on here?" Stephanie demanded.

"What do you mean?" Darcy asked.

"Hey, who are all those people?" Mary asked, glancing up the cliff behind Stephanie.

Stephanie whirled around. Brad was plummeting down toward them with his parents and a bunch of other people from the party. She noticed that Kayla was at Brad's side.

"It's your rescue team," Stephanie said. "Brad and I thought you were drowning." *But instead of being in terrible danger, Darcy was having fun with a Flamingo. And if Mary hadn't started screaming, Brad would have kissed me!*

"This is so embarrassing," Darcy said to the gathering crowd. "I'm sorry you all thought something was wrong." She explained that everything was fine.

Stephanie stood in her dripping clothes, watching Darcy laugh and joke about the mix-up.

Only the joke's on me, she thought, shivering in the cool breeze. Everyone began heading back up the path to the party.

Brad came over to her, followed by Kayla. He handed her a towel.

"That was really brave of you," he told Stephanie. "Jumping in like that to save your friend."

"Thanks." She tried to towel off her hair, but she was totally drenched, too wet for a single towel.

"Steph, you should probably just go home," Kayla said. "Or you're going to freeze."

Stephanie gaped at Kayla. Unbelievable! Kayla was going to use this as a chance to get Stephanie away from Brad.

"Kayla's right," Brad said. "Let me go ask my parents if one of them can drive you home." He dashed up the path after his parents.

"So you and Brad were out on the beach when you heard Mary scream?" Kayla asked, her voice high and tight sounding.

What should I say? Stephanie wondered. She felt torn. Under any other circumstances she'd be totally happy to share the news about Brad with her best friends. He practically kissed her. But Stephanie was afraid it would upset Kayla, and she didn't want Kayla to think she was gloating.

"Uh, yeah," Stephanie said. "We were talking."

"About me?" Kayla asked, brightening.

"No," Stephanie replied. "What makes you think we would talk about you?"

"Because Brad likes me," Kayla declared. "He flirted with me like crazy during the volleyball game. He put an arm around me and hugged me."

Stephanie stared at her friend in disbelief. "Get real, Kayla. Brad was just excited because we beat the Flamingoes. The hug he gave you didn't mean a thing."

Kayla narrowed her eyes. "He hugged me *and* he whispered in my ear that I was great!"

Stephanie rolled her eyes. "You're great at *volleyball*. That's what he meant."

"Look, Steph, you just don't want to admit that he likes me best. Stay away from him."

"No way am I going to stay away from Brad," Stephanie retorted. "Not after he took me for a sunset walk on the beach. And if Mary hadn't started screaming like a fool, he was going to *kiss* me!"

Kayla shook her head so hard that her blond

hair swung over her flushed cheeks. "I can't believe you would lie to me. Especially about something like this!"

Stephanie gasped in shock. "I am not lying."

But Kayla wouldn't listen. "I'm warning you, Steph, Brad is mine."

Kayla turned and marched away. With a sinking feeling in the pit of her stomach, Stephanie watched her friend's back.

First she lost Darcy to a Flamingo. Now, because of their competition over Brad, she had lost Kayla.

What is happening to us? she wondered. *Club Stephanie is falling apart!*

CHAPTER
9

◆ ◄ ◗ ◆

"What were you doing with Mary?" Stephanie demanded early the next morning as soon as Darcy opened her front door.

That question had kept Stephanie awake all night. Had Darcy deserted them? Had she become a Flamingo?

Darcy yawned and slumped against the door frame. "We were surfing."

"You were surfing with a *Flamingo?*" Stephanie still couldn't get over it. "Have you lost your mind?"

Darcy shrugged. "Mary isn't that bad. We've been surfing together a lot."

"She isn't *that* bad?" Stephanie repeated in

shock. She held up a hand and began ticking off the reasons on her fingers one by one. "What about the first Summer Sail session? The Flamingoes almost got us killed on the sailboat. What about the flotilla contest? Mary and the other Flamingoes tried to sabotage our float. What about—"

"You don't have to remind me. I was there." Darcy wrapped her hand around Stephanie's fingers to stop her counting. "The Flamingoes— as a group—did those things. Mary might have helped them, but that's ancient history."

"Yeah, right," Stephanie muttered. Why couldn't Darcy see the problem? "How can you possibly trust Mary for even a minute? For all you know, she's just a Flamingo spy trying to figure out worse tricks to pull on us."

"You're being ridiculous. Mary isn't like that. She's a great surfing buddy. She's teaching me a lot," Darcy assured her.

"She's teaching you to be a Flamingo," Stephanie retorted. "The next thing you know, you'll be wearing pink."

"Oh, please." Darcy rolled her eyes. "All Mary and I do is surf together. We both like it a lot more than sailing. It's not as if we hang out all the time. What's the big deal?"

Stephanie shook her head. "I can't believe I even have to explain that to you. You hate the Flamingoes as much as I do. More, even."

Darcy shrugged. "Well, I like Mary. She's different when she's not with the rest of them."

"I don't think you can be friends with a Flamingo and friends with *me*," Stephanie snapped.

Darcy's eyes widened. Then they narrowed. "You can't tell me who I can be friends with," she informed Stephanie.

Without another word Darcy slammed her front door. Right in Stephanie's face.

Stephanie dreaded going to Summer Sail on Monday. She never heard from Darcy or Kayla all weekend.

Which was just fine with Stephanie.

Only how was she going to get through a day on the boat watching Kayla go after Brad?

"This is absolutely wonderful," Anna said as she raised her arms and stretched.

No, it's not, Stephanie thought. *It's absolutely terrible*. Kayla hadn't spoken to her since they arrived at the marina.

"Do you think we'll spot the dolphin?" Allie wondered.

Josh had told them the marine biologists had

asked all sailors to be on the lookout for the sick dolphin.

"Wouldn't it be cool if we did?" Brad said.

Stephanie sat on one side of Brad, and Kayla sat on the other side. He sat at the tiller while the others ran the sails. All afternoon he had been treating Stephanie as if nothing had happened—as if he had never almost kissed her. In fact, she realized, he was paying as much attention to Kayla as he was to her.

Had she imagined it? she wondered. Did she only *think* he was going to kiss her on the cliff? *Maybe he's just not interested in me anymore. Maybe I did something to offend him.* All Stephanie knew for sure was that she was confused and her stomach was in knots.

Once more she wished she had Darcy to talk things over with. Allie and Anna both told her they didn't want to talk about the Stephanie-Brad-Kayla mess. They said they didn't want to get in the middle.

"Hey, guys! Did you see that?" Anna asked.

Stephanie shifted her attention to Anna, who was on the starboard side of the boat. She was grateful for the distraction.

"What?" Stephanie asked, straining to see where Anna pointed.

95

"It looked like something silver streaking through the water," Anna explained. She raised a hand to shield her eyes from the brightness of the sun and stared harder at the bay. Allie slid up beside Anna.

"There it is again!" Anna cried.

"It's a dolphin!" Allie shrieked.

"Brad, turn to starboard a little," Anna instructed.

"Prepare to come about," Brad replied as the crew got ready to switch sides. "Ready about. Hard-a-lee," he continued as he and the crew switched sides.

Then Stephanie saw the dolphin and pointed. "There it is!"

"Hold the boat steady," Allie ordered.

Everyone stared out over the water, searching for the dolphin.

Suddenly the dolphin lifted its head above the surface of the water and gazed at them. Then abruptly it dove back under the surface, barely making a ripple.

"Did you see that?" Brad asked, awe in his voice.

"It was beautiful," Stephanie commented.

"I've never seen a dolphin up close," Brad told them.

"We haven't either," Kayla informed him. "Unless the dolphins at Sea World count."

They gazed out across the waters for a few minutes longer, but the dolphin didn't resurface.

"I guess it's gone," Allie said.

Suddenly Stephanie had a weird feeling—as if she were being watched. Slowly she turned her head and looked behind her. The dolphin had lifted its head out of the water again and was staring at her! Just a few feet away!

Her breath caught. "It's right here, guys," she said in a low, calm voice. "Don't startle it."

Everyone eased toward the dolphin. The dolphin stayed where it was, the water lapping just below its mouth. It watched everyone in the boat as they watched it.

"This is incredible!" Brad said in a hushed voice.

"It *has* to be the dolphin that the marine biologists are trying to help," Stephanie told them.

"What should we do?" Kayla wondered.

The dolphin moved forward until it was just inches from the boat. It opened its mouth slightly, as though it were smiling at them.

It's so sweet looking, Stephanie thought. She leaned forward and stretched out her hand to pet it. It let out a cry and streaked off like a silver bullet.

Stephanie jerked back, startled by its quick movements.

Brad gazed at her. "Wow. You almost touched it." He sounded awed.

"I didn't mean to frighten it," she told him. She felt terrible that she had caused the dolphin to speed away like that. She never meant to scare the beautiful creature.

"It probably would have left anyway," Anna told her, trying to cheer her up. "After all, it's wild, so it's probably not used to humans."

"It was so beautiful," Allie murmured.

"And it's sick," Stephanie reminded everyone. "We need to let the marine biologists know that we found it."

They trimmed the sails and sped back to the marina. After they had secured the sailboat at the dock, they hurried toward the marina clubhouse.

"Who do we call?" Brad asked.

"Good question," Anna admitted. "I don't imagine we just look up marine biologists in the phone book."

"How about the Bay Wildlife Center?" Stephanie suggested.

"Sounds good," Brad said. He dug into the pocket of his cutoff jeans. "I've got a quarter." He handed it to Stephanie. "You do the talking."

Everyone gathered around her as she phoned the Bay Wildlife Center. When she hung up the phone, she turned to her friends with a huge grin.

"Guess what?" she informed them. "They invited us to go with them to track the dolphin!"

"What are we waiting for?" Anna said. "Let's get back to the docks!"

The group rounded a corner and almost bumped into Darcy and Mary, holding their surfboards.

"Hey, it's the wipeout queen," Brad joked.

"Hi, guys," Darcy said, giving Brad a smile. She glanced at Stephanie and then looked away. Stephanie could tell Darcy was still mad at her.

Which is fine, Stephanie fumed. *Because I'm mad, too. And if Darcy would rather hang out with the Flamingoes, then she's no longer a friend of mine.*

"Isn't Summer Sail over for the day?" Mary asked. "What are you doing heading for the docks?"

There was an awkward silence as Allie, Anna,

Kayla, and Stephanie exchanged uncomfortable looks. *Should we tell them?* Stephanie wondered.

"We're going to look for the sick dolphin," Brad said. "I'm totally psyched. The marine biologists said we could help, since we spotted it."

Darcy's eyes widened. "You actually found the dolphin? That is so cool."

"Can we come along?" Mary asked.

"Sure," Brad answered. "The more the merrier."

"But—" Stephanie began, and then clamped her mouth shut. She didn't want to sound petty in front of Brad. But she didn't want to be on a boat with Darcy and her Flamingo friend.

Stephanie sighed. There was nothing she could do about it now.

This would be a lot more fun if Mary weren't here, Stephanie thought. *Being on a research boat is really cool, and I can't enjoy it because of Darcy and Mary. And Kayla.*

For one thing, Mary and Darcy were completely hogging Brad. He and Darcy were the only ones who would talk to Mary. Stephanie didn't blame Brad, because he didn't know any better and he was nice to everyone.

But Darcy! Stephanie shook her head. Now she knew for sure that Darcy had chosen Mary over

100

her. To make matters worse, Kayla was sulking by the cabin.

Stephanie glanced over at Anna and Allie. They had the right idea. They were concentrating on finding the dolphin. Probably because they didn't know who to talk to!

Suddenly Anna jumped up and waved at one of the marine biologists. "There it is! I see the dolphin!" she shouted. "Oh! It's gone again."

Stephanie hurried up to the bow to join her friend. "Where?" she asked. She peered at the water. "Ohhh!"

The dolphin popped its head out of the water and squeaked. Then it dove back under again.

"It's like the dolphin's trying to talk," Kayla said.

"I hope the boat doesn't frighten it," Stephanie murmured.

The head of the research team, an older man named Dr. Harris, stood by Stephanie. "Wonderful. He's still here. Matt, do you have the medicine ready?"

A man in his twenties kneeling on the far side of the boat looked over. "Almost," he replied.

"Would you mind helping Matt?" Dr. Harris asked Stephanie. "We want to do this as quickly as possible."

"Sure!" Stephanie hurried over to Matt and knelt down beside him. "What do I need to do?"

"Take one of the pills out of that jar," he instructed.

Stephanie picked up one of the pills. It was almost the same size as the tip of her finger. "What is this?" she asked.

"Antibiotics for the dolphin," Matt answered.

"What's it going to do—swallow this with a glass of water?" Stephanie joked. She couldn't imagine how they could get the dolphin to take the little pill.

Matt laughed. "No, the dolphin is going to swallow it with a fish."

Matt reached into a nearby bucket and pulled out a fish. Gently he bent the fish's head back until its gills spread open. "Slip the pill through the gills."

Stephanie shuddered when her fingers touched the cold scales of the fish, but she pushed the pill past its gills.

"Good job," Matt said as he stood. Stephanie followed him to the railing. "Do you want to give the dolphin his first dose of medicine?"

Stephanie's heart pounded excitedly. "You bet!" She took the fish from him, ignoring its slimy coldness. She leaned over the railing and extended her arm.

"Don't be disappointed if he won't take the fish," Matt cautioned her. "If he's really sick, he might not."

"I understand." Holding her breath, she waited. She hoped that the dolphin would let her feed him. Then suddenly—it happened. The dolphin leaped out of the water like a silver streak and snatched the fish right out of her hand! She let out a gasp. She had seen dolphins fed that way at Sea World, but nothing had prepared her for the thrill of having a wild dolphin eat from her hand. "He took the fish!" she cried.

Her friends clapped and cheered, and Matt smiled broadly. "Come on, we need to give him some more antibiotics and some vitamins."

Stephanie and her friends helped Matt prepare more fish. They took turns feeding the dolphin. Stephanie was amazed by how tame the dolphin seemed, but Matt explained that in most circumstances dolphins liked human company.

"This is just too cool," Kayla said as they stood by the railing after they had given the dolphin all the medication.

"But the dolphin is still stuck here in the bay," Stephanie said worriedly.

"Just watch," Matt promised. "We'll help him get back to his pals."

They watched as the research team threw a net out over the water—and over the dolphin!

"Oh, no!" Anna cried. "They're going to frighten it."

Stephanie heard a splash. Matt had jumped into the water and was swimming toward the dolphin. "What's he doing?" Stephanie asked Dr. Harris, who had moved in beside her.

"Matt will try to calm the dolphin. Once it's ready, we'll bring the dolphin on board and cart it out to the sea."

"That is so great," Stephanie said. The dolphin really seemed to like Matt, who was doing a good job of keeping the dolphin from getting too scared. Stephanie watched in amazement as the dolphin was finally hoisted into the air and brought over the railing. The biologists set it down on a padded floor.

Dr. Harris hurried over to the dolphin and quickly wrapped it in a sheet. "Stephanie, I need you and your friend to get over here—quickly!"

Stephanie's breath caught. Dr. Harris pointed at Mary—and Mary certainly wasn't Stephanie's friend. But the urgency in Dr. Harris's voice stopped her from telling him that. This was too important. She and Mary rushed over to Dr. Harris.

"I've wrapped a sheet around it to keep him moist and cool," Dr. Harris explained, "but I need you to take those buckets and pour water over it until we get farther out to sea."

"Yes, sir," Stephanie and Mary said together.

They grabbed the buckets, dipped them into the bay, brought them up, and poured the water over the dolphin.

"I didn't realize they would bring the dolphin on board," Mary said.

"I just thought they'd lead it out of the bay and into the ocean," Stephanie admitted.

Mary glanced up at Stephanie. "You know, Darcy is really upset."

Stephanie stared at Mary. Darcy talked to a Flamingo about their fight? She poured more water onto the dolphin, trying to ignore Mary.

"You're being really hard on her," Mary continued. "And I think you are being totally unfair."

"And I think you should mind your own business," Stephanie snapped. She felt her cheeks flush with anger.

"You are being such a baby," Mary said. "So

what if Darcy and I go surfing. You're still her best friend."

Stephanie bit her lip and continued pouring water on the dolphin. She glanced over to where Darcy was sitting. Stephanie had to admit that Darcy looked kind of miserable.

"Just because I'm friends with Darah doesn't mean I can't be friends with Darcy, too," Mary said. "And the same thing goes for Darcy. Why don't you get that?"

Stephanie gazed down at the dolphin. "Maybe I have been overreacting," she admitted. Then she looked at Mary. "But you have played some pretty mean tricks on me—you and the Flamingoes."

Now it was Mary who stared down at the dolphin, concentrating on keeping it wet. "Yeah, I know. We've been pretty dumb sometimes."

Stephanie was surprised to hear Mary admit that the Flamingoes were anything less than perfect. And she genuinely seemed to care about Darcy and Darcy's feelings.

Stephanie didn't think Flamingoes ever cared about anything except their own popularity.

Could Darcy be right? Could Mary actually be kind of okay?

"You know, Mary," Stephanie said. "I think you're right about a bunch of things."

Stephanie smiled at Mary. She'd never expected that she might like a Flamingo—just a little. Mary grinned back.

Dr. Harris came over to them. "Thanks, girls," Dr. Harris said. "We're going to put it back in the water now."

Mary and Stephanie joined the others and watched the rescue team lower the dolphin back into the bay.

Once freed of the netting, the dolphin swam around the boat. Then it raised itself out of the water, balanced on its tail, and gave a gawking cry.

Stephanie thought she could actually see it smile.

Then it dove into the water, came back up, and streaked out to sea.

As the boat made its way back to the docks, Stephanie hurried over to Darcy. She felt a sharp pang when Darcy gave her a wary look. *She thinks we're going to have another fight*, Stephanie realized.

She took a deep breath. "Darcy, I'm really, really sorry," she said. "I was out of line telling you to choose between me and Mary."

An enormous grin spread across Darcy's face. "So you came back to your senses," she teased. "I knew you would." She gave Stephanie a quick hug.

Stephanie felt so much better.

The boat finished docking, and everyone disembarked.

Just then a young woman with a camera ran up to the group. "I just heard the news on the coast guard radio. Is it true? Did you guys really help rescue the dolphin?"

"They sure did," Dr. Harris answered.

"Excellent! Mind if I get a picture of you all for the marina newsletter?"

"Awesome!" Stephanie said. "What do you think, guys?"

"Yeah! Let's do it!" Darcy agreed. She slung an arm around Stephanie's shoulders for the photo. Mary stood next to them.

This is great. My problems with Darcy are over, Stephanie thought as the young woman snapped the picture. She smiled her biggest, happiest smile.

Until she caught sight of Kayla with her arm wrapped around Brad's waist.

My problems with Darcy are over, she corrected herself, *but my problems with Kayla are as bad as ever!*

CHAPTER
10

◆ ◀ ◗ ◆

Why does she *have to be early, too?* Stephanie thought when she noticed Kayla locking her bicycle at the rack the next morning.

Stephanie ignored Kayla and strolled past the marina clubhouse to the Snack Shack. The Snack Shack was a large booth where food and drinks were sold. Behind the booth were patio tables. Hardly anyone was around.

Stephanie walked up to the counter. "A banana-strawberry smoothie and a granola bar, please," she ordered from the high-school guy behind the counter.

"I'll have a fresh-squeezed orange juice and a corn muffin," Kayla said behind her.

Stephanie watched the guy in the booth slicing the bananas for her shake. Then he sliced the strawberries. It seemed like he was taking forever. She put the money on the counter so she could make a quick getaway.

She was very aware of Kayla standing silently behind her and could practically feel Kayla's eyes burning into her.

"Sorry, have to get more yogurt." The guy grinned and vanished through the door.

Stephanie didn't want to stand there waiting with Kayla. She paced to the edge of the booth and glanced around the side.

Her heart stopped. Darah sat at the nearest table with her back to the Snack Shack counter. There was no way Stephanie could miss her—not with all that flowing auburn hair, all-pink outfit, and monogrammed backpack.

And she was sitting with Brad!

Stephanie ducked back behind the Snack Shack booth.

Oh, no, she groaned to herself. *Was Darah after Brad, too?*

"Hey, do you want your smoothie?" the guy from the Snack Shack called.

"Huh?" Stephanie had trouble taking her eyes off Brad and Darah.

"Earth to Stephanie!" Kayla said. She walked over to Stephanie and handed her the shake and granola bar. "What is wrong with you?"

Kayla peered around the Snack Shack to where Stephanie was looking and gasped. "What are *they* doing together?"

Stephanie shook her head. "I don't know. But I thought it was weird that Darah *wasn't* going after Brad. She always tries to steal the guys I like."

"We like," Kayla reminded her.

Darah tossed her hair and laughed at something Brad said. He draped an arm across the back of her chair.

"They look very friendly," Kayla commented.

"Too friendly," Stephanie agreed. She stopped. "Shhh! They're talking! If we're quiet, I'll be able to hear them from here."

Kayla nodded.

"Cough it up, Darah," Stephanie heard Brad say. "I won, and you know it."

Stephanie blinked in confusion. What was Brad talking about? What had he won?

"I beg to differ, cousin," Darah said in a sickly sweet voice. "You haven't won yet."

Cousin! Stephanie and Kayla exchanged horrified glances. Brad and Darah were *cousins?*

"You still have to pull off the final stage of the bet, and I am *sooo* looking forward to that. Who do Stephanie and her little friends think they are, saving that dolphin and getting themselves into the marina newsletter?" Darah asked. "The Flamingoes should be on the front page instead."

"Well, don't worry, you'll get your revenge soon enough. Stephanie and Kayla are both totally nuts for me," Brad bragged. "And they are barely speaking to each other."

Darah giggled. "I know. All my friends in Summer Sail are having so much fun watching them trip over themselves to impress you."

Stephanie felt her stomach twist in horror. How many people were in on the dare? She wanted the ground to open up and swallow her.

"It looks like Stephanie's little club is breaking up," Darah gloated. "Darcy seems to be out of the picture. Kayla and Stephanie hate each other." Darah smiled. "It's great. They'll never be a bother to me or my friends again!"

"Your final plan for the dance may be kind of hard to pull off," Brad cautioned.

"That's why I'm betting you big bucks that you can do it," Darah teased.

"Getting Stephanie and Kayla to agree to go

to the dance with me will be easy," Brad boasted. "But keeping them from finding out about each other until the perfect moment will be tough."

"But that's the bet, Brad." Darah wagged a finger at him. "You get them *both* to be your date. I announce that you are crowned the Merman King. Then I'll ask your Mermaid Queen to come out." Darah started laughing. "What a great scene. I can just picture it. Kayla and Stephanie will both come out, and they'll probably start a fight right there in front of everybody. If we can get them both to embarrass themselves in the same night, you win. *And* you get the money."

Brad threw his head back and laughed. "Perfect."

Stephanie felt Kayla stiffen behind her. Kayla started to move toward Darah and Brad's table.

Stephanie grabbed her friend's arm. She put a finger to her mouth and shook her head. Now was not the time to let Darah and Brad know that they were on to their little dare. They backed away from the Snack Shack and headed toward the marina.

"Can you believe it?" Stephanie asked. "I've

never been so angry in my life! I thought he was my Mr. Perfect!"

"He is as far from perfect as a person can be," Kayla fumed. "He's a Flamingo!"

"Or as close to being a Flamingo as a *guy* can get," Stephanie agreed.

"And everyone at Summer Sail knows about the bet!" Kayla wailed.

"That's not the worst part," Stephanie realized. "Not only were Darah and Brad making fools of us, but we were making fools of each other. All this is really our fault. We let a guy come between us and our friendship."

"I'm so sorry, Steph," Kayla apologized. "I should have stayed away from Brad once I realized you liked him."

"I'm sorry, too. Your friendship is more important than getting a boyfriend. I didn't realize that until now," Stephanie explained. "Let's agree never to let a boy come between us again!"

"Agreed!" Kayla cried without hesitation. "So what do we do now?"

Stephanie's eyes glittered. "We work together to get our revenge—against Darah and Brad!"

CHAPTER
11

◆ ◀ ◖ ◆

"This is so humiliating," Stephanie told her friends later that night. She covered her face with her pillow. Kayla, Darcy, Anna, and Allie sat in Stephanie's bedroom. They were trying to come up with some way to get revenge on Darah and Brad.

"It's the worst trick the Flamingoes have pulled so far," Kayla agreed.

"And they almost got away with it," Darcy exclaimed.

"I can't believe that Brad turned out to be such a jerk," Allie said. "He was so nice."

"I know," Stephanie groaned from under her pillow. She tossed it aside. "I thought he was Mr. Perfect."

"He was," Kayla commented. "Mr. Perfect Nightmare."

"Speaking of perfect nightmares, did you ever consider the fact that your Flamingo friend, Mary, might be in on this little scheme of Darah's?" Stephanie asked.

"She isn't in on anything," Darcy insisted. "How could she be? Mary and I have spent every moment we can surfing. She hasn't hung out with the Flamingoes in days."

Stephanie frowned. *I guess that's true*, Stephanie admitted to herself. *I guess Mary really doesn't have anything to do with this.*

"So what are we going to do to take care of Darah and her creepy cousin?" Darcy flopped down beside Stephanie on the bed.

Stephanie couldn't help but smile. It felt great to have all her friends together with no one fighting. She was sure the five of them would find some way to get back at the Flamingoes.

"The next time we go sailing, we could toss Brad into the bay and make him swim back to shore," Kayla suggested.

"That's harsh enough only if the bay is full of sharks when we dump him in," Stephanie joked. Then she became more serious. "Darah's main objective is to humiliate us," Stephanie told the others. "We need to do something that will humiliate Darah."

"And Brad," Kayla said.

"Definitely."

"It has to take place on the Under-the-Stars Midnight Cruise," Darcy murmured. "We have to turn the joke around on them."

"If Brad asks me to that stupid dance, I'm going to tell him just what I think of him!" Kayla declared.

Stephanie smiled as a plan began to form in her head. "Oh, no, you're not," she informed Kayla. "You're going to act as if you are totally thrilled to be his date."

"Why would I do that when I don't like him anymore?" Kayla asked, confused.

"Because I'll agree also."

Kayla creased her brows. "But then he and Darah will win the bet. And they'll make us look like total fools."

Stephanie's smile grew brighter. "No, they won't. Because we're going to make sure that things don't go exactly the way they've planned."

"You have an idea, don't you?" Darcy said, a sly grin forming on her lips.

Stephanie gazed at each of her friends. "Do I ever! And it's really, really good!"

The Under-the-Stars Midnight Cruise was held on the huge Summer Sail session sailboat—the *Sunshine*.

Stephanie arrived with Brad. She wore her favorite outfit, a clingy silver tank dress with a black choker.

Stephanie gazed over at Brad. *He looks sooo handsome tonight,* she thought. He wore a brown sport jacket and neatly pressed khakis.

For a moment Stephanie wished the night could end differently. She wished there had been no dare and that Brad was still her Mr. Perfect. *But he's not,* she reminded herself firmly. *This isn't a real date at all—it's revenge!*

"I hope they have plenty of food," Brad said as they strolled onto the deck. "I'm starving."

"You're always starving," Stephanie teased. She didn't want Brad to have any idea that she was on to him. She wanted him to believe she was still crazy about him.

Just the way I thought he was crazy about me, she thought sadly. She forced herself to smile brightly. "The decorations are beautiful," she added, glancing around.

"Darah worked on the cruise and dance committee. She did a terrific job," Brad told her.

"Do you know Darah Judson very well?" Stephanie asked, imitating the sweet innocent voice she'd heard Darah use so often.

"She and I—" Brad stopped short.

Stephanie smiled sweetly, certain he was about to slip up and tell her they were cousins. "She and you . . ." she prompted.

"We talked a little during Summer Sail," Brad said.

He nervously pulled on the ends of his jacket. Then he glanced at his watch. "Listen, why don't you wait here and I'll get us something to drink?"

"I'll go with you," she offered, knowing he was looking for an excuse to leave—so he could pick up his second date, Kayla.

"Oh, no," he said. "There's bound to be a line at the punch bowl. You stay here. Enjoy the music and the decorations." He hurried away before she could protest.

"Why, hello, Stephanie!"

Stephanie turned at the irritating sound of Darah's voice.

"Hi, Darah." Stephanie smiled her sweetest, most fake smile.

"Did I just see you with Brad?" Darah asked.

Stephanie nodded. "He's my date tonight."

"Brad seems to be the sweetest guy," Darah observed. "You are so lucky that *you're* his girlfriend."

"Actually, Darah, I do feel lucky tonight. Very lucky." Stephanie stifled a giggle, thinking of the plan she and her friends had worked out.

Darah walked away in her long, pink satin dress with the puffy, pink-and-white-striped skirt. *Stephanie, you are brilliant,* she congratulated herself.

Half the night went by before Stephanie saw Brad again. She had anticipated his being missing in action while he picked up Kayla and the two of them had dinner. But still, Stephanie couldn't help feeling annoyed at his absence.

Just then she caught sight of Brad's brown blazer out of the corner of her eye. "Brad! You're back!" she called. She rushed to his side.

He handed her a drink. "Sorry it took me so long. They ran out of punch and said it wouldn't take long to get some more, so I waited. My mistake," he explained.

Stephanie forced herself not to roll her eyes. Not only was Brad lying—he was a terrible liar. She knew that Kayla had led him straight to the cruise buffet as soon as they'd arrived.

"I'm just glad you're finally here. I'm *starving.*" She slipped her arm through his. "And you must be really famished, too!"

"Uh, I'm not really *that* hungry," he began.

She slapped his arm teasingly. "Oh, Brad, stop kidding. You were ready to hit the buffet line as soon as we got here."

"Well . . . uh . . ."

But Stephanie continued. "Come on, silly. We'll share a plate."

"*Share* a plate?" Brad's face brightened. "Okay."

Stephanie smiled mishievously. If Kayla had followed through on their plan, she knew that Brad had already eaten a full meal and was probably stuffed.

Sure, Stephanie thought. The idea of sharing a plate didn't *seem* bad—but Brad didn't know what she had in store for him.

She led him to the dining room and made him hold her plate while she heaped it with food: shrimp, fish, fries, corn on the cob. She took two helpings of everything.

"I think you're getting too much, Stephanie." He moved the plate aside when she started to heap mashed potatoes on it.

121

"Don't be silly, Brad. We need to eat now so we'll have plenty of energy to dance all night."

With the way she and Kayla were stuffing him full of food—and then planning to run him ragged, he'd probably end up nauseated before the night was over. *Good*, Stephanie thought. *That's the least he deserves.* She pulled the plate back and piled potatoes on it.

"Why don't we sit over by the railing?" Stephanie suggested. "It's so romantic."

Brad followed her, glancing around nervously. He sat very close to her. Stephanie knew that it wasn't because he liked her. It was probably because he figured Kayla would have a harder time spotting him that way.

Stephanie picked up her fork and nudged the plate toward Brad. "Dig in," she ordered.

He gave her a weak smile, took a deep breath, and speared a shrimp.

She watched Brad chew slowly. Very slowly. He swallowed. Stephanie thought he looked like he was in pain.

Time to start putting on the heat and make him really uncomfortable, she coached herself.

"Have you seen Kayla around tonight?" Stephanie asked. "My friends told me she brought a fabulous date to the dance. I'd really like to meet him. Wouldn't you?"

Brad started to choke. Stephanie hid her grin from him as she pounded on his back. He reached for a glass of water and took a swallow. "I'm sure we'll run into them eventually," he said, covering as well as he could.

"You're probably right." Stephanie wiped her mouth with the linen napkin and shoved the plate in front of Brad. "Here. The rest is all for you." She smiled at him sweetly. "I know what a big appetite you have."

Later, as Stephanie stood in the ladies' room with Kayla, Allie, and Anna, she checked her watch. Almost midnight. "Is everyone ready to put our plan into action?" she asked her friends.

"Absolutely." Kayla nodded.

Stephanie glanced at herself in the bathroom mirror. She reapplied her lip gloss. "Remember, we have to make sure Brad doesn't know we suspect anything."

Kayla shook her head. "I can't believe we've managed to pull this off so far. I've wanted to scream at him so many times tonight."

"I know," Stephanie agreed.

"It makes me so mad that he thinks he's getting away with this horrible bet. He is so proud of himself for fooling us. What a jerk." Anna seethed.

"Well, at least you've been making him miserable the whole time—running him around like a maniac," Allie declared, smoothing her hair into place.

Stephanie giggled. "He is so worn out from dancing with me and Kayla that he looks like he ran a marathon."

"And all that food." Kayla snickered. "Between us both practically force-feeding him and then making him dance, I'm surprised he hasn't barfed."

"Well, the worst is yet to come," Anna declared. "Allie and I have everything in place on our end. The last two parts of our plan are guaranteed to go smoothly."

"Excellent." Stephanie smiled at her reflection. "Before the night is over, Brad and Darah will both find out what it feels like to be humiliated."

"And they'll know that they didn't pull anything over on us!" Kayla agreed.

"Too bad Darcy isn't here." Stephanie sighed. She slipped her lip gloss into her evening purse. "She'd love to be in on this prank."

"Only Summer Sail kids are allowed on the cruise," Kayla reminded her.

Stephanie fluffed her hair one final time. "Well, ready or not, Flamingoes, here we come!"

She, Kayla, and the rest of her friends slapped high-fives, then left the bathroom.

Kayla slipped away and Stephanie scanned the crowd for Brad.

First, she reminded herself, *I have to get my ammunition.* She hurried over to the refreshment table and poured herself a big glass of cranberry juice.

She checked her watch again. Darah was going to make her announcement at midnight. Stephanie had only ten minutes to put part two of the plan into action. Would she be able to find Brad in time?

Stephanie noticed him weaving his way through the crowd toward her. *Right on schedule,* she thought to herself. *Time to go into my oh-Brad-you're-so-wonderful act. And try not to gag.* She quickly crossed the deck to meet him.

"Miss me?" she asked as she gazed up at Brad.

"Of course I did," he told her.

Stephanie bit her tongue so that nothing nasty would slip out.

"Let's dance some more," she suggested. "You

are *such* a good dancer." Before he could say anything, she grabbed his arm with her free hand. She pulled him toward the dance floor.

Okay. Now, as soon as it is crowded enough, she told herself, *go for it. Ready, set . . .*

"Oops!" Stephanie spilled the full glass of cranberry juice all over Brad's khakis.

"Hey!" he exclaimed, jumping back.

Good job, Stephanie congratulated herself. *You drenched him!* "Oh, Brad, I am so sorry! I can't believe I was so clumsy. Someone bumped my arm and—"

"It's okay. It was an accident." He looked toward the refreshment table. Stephanie could see him fighting back his annoyance. He gave her a tight smile. "I guess I should get some napkins."

"No! That won't be good enough. You have to wash your pants out right away!" she told him. "Cranberry juice stains really badly."

"But what can I do?" Brad said. He glanced down at the large stain. The dark liquid continued spreading across the light fabric. Stephanie knew Brad was worrying the juice would make him look dumb in front of everyone.

"It's my fault," Stephanie said. "Let me take

126

care of it." She grabbed his hand and dragged him off the dance floor.

"What are you going to do?" he demanded.

Stephanie pretended she couldn't hear him over the music. She brought him behind a row of Japanese screens that had been set up at the back of the deck.

Josh told Stephanie earlier that the portion of the deck behind the screens was off limits to the party-goers. Stephanie checked her watch again. Only a few minutes until Darah's big announcement.

"Why did you shove me behind here?" he demanded.

"Take off your pants," Stephanie ordered.

"What?" Brad stared at Stephanie as though she were crazy.

"Give them to me and I'll rinse out the cran-berry juice. It's the only way to keep the stain from setting. Then I'll blot the pants dry with napkins and towels. You'll be clean and all set to go in just five minutes." Stephanie slipped over to the other side of the screens.

"I don't know . . ." Brad hesitated.

"Please, Brad," Stephanie begged. "I'll feel so terrible if I've ruined your pants. It's the least I can do."

Hurry up and do it, she urged him silently. *We're running out of time!*

Brad handed the wet khakis to Stephanie over the screen.

"Now, you don't worry about a thing," Stephanie said, her voice dripping with sweetness. "I'll take care of everything."

She tossed the pants to the side and dashed back to the party. She arrived just in time to see Darah heading for the podium.

Stephanie scanned the room. Anna and Allie caught her attention. They pointed to an ornate golden crown sitting on the stage. Then each of them gave her the thumbs-up sign. Everything was going perfectly.

Darah tapped on the microphone. Then she leaned into it and addressed the crowd. "The time has come for the big announcement. Crowning the Merman King and the Mermaid Queen of Summer Sail!"

Everyone applauded. *Here it comes,* Stephanie thought. *The big moment.*

Darah shot a look at Tiffany and Cynthia. They grinned at her. A wicked smile crossed Darah's face. Stephanie knew it was because Darah thought her moment of triumph had arrived.

Will she *be surprised,* Stephanie thought.

"I am pleased to announce that Brad Miller is our Merman King," Darah declared. "Brad, please come up and claim your crown!" She glanced around the deck. "Oh, Brad? Where are you, Brad?"

A murmur rippled through the crowd as everyone gazed around, trying to locate Brad.

Stephanie could see Darah's jaw tighten. Clearly she was becoming impatient. Stephanie snickered. *Darah's really bugged that this isn't going according to her plan.*

"Brad," Darah repeated. She sounded annoyed. "Does anyone know where Brad is?"

"I do!" Stephanie shouted. She turned and walked toward the Japanese screens on the deck. Everyone turned to see where she was going.

"Here's our very own King Merman!" Stephanie folded one of the screens back, revealing Brad. He stood in total shock, dressed only in his shirt and underwear.

Everyone started to laugh. Some people hooted. Several pointed.

Brad's face turned the shade of a Flamingo.

"Gee, Brad," Stephanie said. "Looks like you've learned a valuable lesson: Never make a bet with a Flamingo. You'll always end up losing."

Then Stephanie turned back toward the stage to face Darah.

The Flamingo's eyes narrowed. "Our little ceremony isn't over quite yet," she declared. "We still need to crown our Mermaid Queen."

Stephanie shook her head. Darah was determined to embarrass Stephanie and Kayla, and she didn't even care if she took her own cousin down with them.

"Since Brad is the king, his date shall be his queen," Darah announced dramatically. "Now, will his queen please step forward."

No one moved.

Darah walked down from the stage. She stood close to Stephanie. "Come on, we know Brad didn't come to the dance alone. Who is Brad's queen?"

"You are!" Kayla shouted. She dashed through the crowd and picked up the crown Allie and Anna planted on the stage. She raced over to Stephanie, and together, the two of them shoved the crown down on Darah's head.

Splat! Black goop oozed down Darah's gorgeous auburn hair.

Stephanie laughed. Allie and Anna had done a *great* job putting the smelly, sticky machine oil on the inside of the crown!

"Aaaggghh!" Darah shrieked. "My hair!"

The thick black gunk trailed down Darah's pink chiffon dress, leaving a puddle on the floor. "My dress!" she screamed.

Around her, everyone exploded in a new fit of laughter.

Kayla threw an arm around Stephanie's shoulders. "Well, this is really interesting," she began. "It looks like we won our bet after all, Steph!"

"B-bet?" Darah yelled, her voice shaking with anger. "What bet?"

"Oh, you see, Kayla and I had a bet," Stephanie explained. "She bet me that we couldn't embarrass both you and your *cousin*, *Brad*, on the same night."

"You—how did you find out . . . ?" Darah demanded.

Stephanie smiled at Kayla. Then she felt another arm rest on her shoulders. She turned. Anna and Allie were standing on the other side of her, supporting her.

She turned back to Darah. "How we found out isn't important. What *is* important is the fact that we all had a bet." Stephanie stepped up close to Darah. "What do you think, Darah? Who won? I would say that *we* did. And that *you* lost. Big-time."

CHAPTER
12

♦ ◄ ◣ ♦

That night Stephanie, Allie, Anna, and Kayla gathered at Kayla's house. The doorbell rang and Darcy burst through the front door.

"You have to tell me what happened!" Darcy said, breathless. "I ran over here to find out. Now spill! Every detail!"

"It was great," Stephanie reported. She took a brownie from the tray in front of her. "Darah finally got what she deserved."

"Seeing Darah crowned Queen Disaster was definitely the highlight of the summer," Kayla said.

"And Brad!" Anna laughed so hard, she started snorting.

"His face was as red as a cooked lobster." Allie giggled.

"Well, my face was red when I realized Brad was dating me on a bet!" Stephanie exclaimed. "I really liked him. And he made me think he liked me."

"Me, too," Kayla admitted.

"He certainly wasn't Mr. Perfect," Darcy told them.

"That's for sure. Far from it." Stephanie took a sip of her lemonade. "I'm glad you're here, Darcy."

"Where else would I be?" Darcy picked up a brownie.

Stephanie shrugged. "Well, you know . . ."

"I like going surfing with Mary," Darcy said. "But there's no way I would miss one of our Friday night sleepovers! Mary's a good friend, but she could never replace all of you."

The girls clinked brownies in agreement.

"I think Darah finally figured out that no matter what she does, she can't keep us from being friends," Stephanie declared.

"I don't know." Allie shook her head. "I have a feeling Darah never learns anything for very long."

Anna sighed. "I hate to say it, but Allie's probably right. Just because we got Darah good this time doesn't mean we can forget about the Flamingoes."

"We can forget about them tonight, at least," Kayla said. "Please?"

"Deal!" The girls all nodded at one another.

"Hey, Stephanie." Darcy poured a big glass of milk and dunked her brownie into it. "Now that the summer is over, do you still believe in fate?"

Stephanie chewed on her brownie, thinking over the events of the summer.

Each time she thought she had found her Mr. Perfect, she was wrong. Each time she tried to make sure that she was following her destiny, nothing went the way she had expected.

"You know," Stephanie told her friends with a grin, "I still believe there's one guy out there I'm destined to be with. There's still a perfect guy for me."

"Oh, brother," Anna moaned.

"But from now on," Stephanie finished, "I think I'm going to leave fate—up to fate!"

"Whew!" Allie breathed a sigh.

"At least," said Stephanie, smiling at her friends, "until next summer!"

FULL HOUSE Stephanie™

PHONE CALL FROM A FLAMINGO	88004-7/$3.99
THE BOY-OH-BOY NEXT DOOR	88121-3/$3.99
TWIN TROUBLES	88290-2/$3.99
HIP HOP TILL YOU DROP	88291-0/$3.99
HERE COMES THE BRAND NEW ME	89858-2/$3.99
THE SECRET'S OUT	89859-0/$3.99
DADDY'S NOT-SO-LITTLE GIRL	89860-4/$3.99
P.S. FRIENDS FOREVER	89861-2/$3.99
GETTING EVEN WITH THE FLAMINGOES	52273-6/$3.99
THE DUDE OF MY DREAMS	52274-4/$3.99
BACK-TO-SCHOOL COOL	52275-2/$3.99
PICTURE ME FAMOUS	52276-0/$3.99
TWO-FOR-ONE CHRISTMAS FUN	53546-3/$3.99
THE BIG FIX-UP MIX-UP	53547-1/$3.99
TEN WAYS TO WRECK A DATE	53548-X/$3.99
WISH UPON A VCR	53549-8/$3.99
DOUBLES OR NOTHING	56841-8/$3.99
SUGAR AND SPICE ADVICE	56842-6/$3.99
NEVER TRUST A FLAMINGO	56843-4/$3.99
THE TRUTH ABOUT BOYS	00361-5/$3.99
CRAZY ABOUT THE FUTURE	00362-3/$3.99
MY SECRET ADMIRER	00363-1/$3.99
BLUE RIBBON CHRISTMAS	00830-7/$3.99
THE STORY ON OLDER BOYS	00831-5/$3.99
MY THREE WEEKS AS A SPY	00832-3/$3.99
NO BUSINESS LIKE SHOW BUSINESS	01725-X/$3.99

 Available from Minstrel® Books Published by Pocket Books

FULL HOUSE™
Michelle

#5: THE GHOST IN MY CLOSET 53573-0/$3.99

#6: BALLET SURPRISE 53574-9/$3.99

#7: MAJOR LEAGUE TROUBLE 53575-7/$3.99

#8: MY FOURTH-GRADE MESS 53576-5/$3.99

#9: BUNK 3, TEDDY, AND ME 56834-5/$3.99

#10: MY BEST FRIEND IS A MOVIE STAR!
(Super Edition) 56835-3/$3.99

#11: THE BIG TURKEY ESCAPE 56836-1/$3.99

#12: THE SUBSTITUTE TEACHER 00364-X/$3.99

#13: CALLING ALL PLANETS 00365-8/$3.99

#14: I'VE GOT A SECRET 00366-6/$3.99

#15: HOW TO BE COOL 00833-1/$3.99

#16: THE NOT-SO-GREAT OUTDOORS 00835-8/$3.99

#17: MY HO-HO-HORRIBLE CHRISTMAS 00836-6/$3.99

MY AWESOME HOLIDAY FRIENDSHIP BOOK
(An Activity Book) 00840-4/$3.99

FULL HOUSE MICHELLE OMNIBUS 02181-8/$6.99

#18: MY ALMOST PERFECT PLAN 00837-4/$3.99

#19: APRIL FOOLS 01729-2/$3.99

A MINSTREL® BOOK
Published by Pocket Books

Simon & Schuster Mail Order Dept. BWB
200 Old Tappan Rd., Old Tappan, N.J. 07675

Please send me the books I have checked above. I am enclosing $_____(please add $0.75 to cover the postage and handling for each order. Please add appropriate sales tax). Send check or money order--no cash or C.O.D.'s please. Allow up to six weeks for delivery. For purchase over $10.00 you may use VISA: card number, expiration date and customer signature must be included.

Name _____

Address _____

City _____ State/Zip _____

VISA Card # _____ Exp.Date _____

Signature _____

1033-26

Meet the Walker sisters:
Rose, Daisy, Laurel, and Lily

THE YEAR
I TURNED
Sixteen

Four sisters. Four stories.

#1 Rose

"Being the oldest of three sisters has never been easy, but it was especially hard the year I turned sixteen. That was the year that the things I thought would always be the same changed forever."

#2 Daisy
(Coming mid-August 1998)

#3 Laurel
(Coming mid-October 1998)

#4 Lily
(Coming mid-December 1998)

A brand-new book series
by Diane Schwemm

Available from Archway Paperbacks
Published by Pocket Books

2006

FULL HOUSE™

Club Stephanie

Summer is here and Stephanie is ready for some fun!

A brand-new miniseries! Collect all three books.

#1 Fun, Sun, and Flamingoes

#2 Fireworks and Flamingoes

#3 Flamingo Revenge

-All Now Available-

Based on the hit Warner Bros. TV series!

A MINSTREL BOOK

Published by Pocket Books

1357-03